Memoirs of a Madman

D0815137

Memoirs of a Madman

Gustave Flaubert

Translated by Andrew Brown

ET REMOTISSIMA PROPE

100 PAGES

100 PAGES
Published by Hesperus Press Limited
4 Rickett Street, London sw6 1RU
www.hesperuspress.com

First published by Hesperus Press Limited, 2002

Introduction and English language translation © Andrew Brown, 2002
Foreword © Germaine Greer, 2002

Designed and typeset by Fraser Muggeridge
Printed in the United Arab Emirates by Oriental Press

ISBN: 1-84391-000-4

CONTENTS

FOREWORD

There was never a time when Gustave Flaubert did not think of himself as a writer. He had thirty playlets to his credit before he was ten years old. At boarding-school in Rouen from the age of eleven, he whiled away the long evenings by writing all kinds of short fictions, 'opuscules historiques', and another play, spun out of his escapist reading and the morbid fantasies of his loneliness. *Memoirs of a Madman,* written before he was sixteen, is his twenty-fifth surviving work. His hero is a younger version of himself and the narrator an older version of that self, but the disillusionment and disgust that he gives vent to can be found in the letters written to his chum Ernest Charpentier by Flaubert when he was not yet fourteen.

During his life Flaubert forbade the publication of his juvenilia; the text of *Memoirs of a Madman* was not published until December 1900 since which time academics have mined it for information about the personality of a great artist, using it as the kind of factual account of events that might be extracted during sessions with a psychoanalyst, rather than understanding not only that the sixteen-year-old Flaubert shaped his account in a self-consciously literary fashion but that he had been modelling his actual behaviour on literary precedents for years. 'I recall with what intense pleasure I devoured, at that time, the pages of Byron and of *Werther*, with what transports I read *Hamlet*, *Romeo*, and the most ardent productions of our period, all those works, in a word, which make the soul melt with rapture or set it afire with enthusiasm.'

The boy who was in Trouville on a family holiday in 1836

had already cast himself as a Hamlet figure, 'like John-a-dreams', condemned by his own 'bourgeoisophobia' to inhabit a fantasy world of superior pleasures. In Chapter 10 of *Memoirs of a Madman* he recounts how, instead of playing with other children, he went for long Byronic walks along the shore, and just happened to find himself beyond the village, at the place where bathers of both sexes came to the beach in bathrobes, which they left at the water's edge while they swam in their underwear. At the water's edge he finds a red pelisse with black stripes and moves it out of reach of the water. The artfulness of his way of recounting the series of events is worth noting: 'That day a charming red pelisse with black stripes had been left on the shore. The tide was rising – the shore was festooned with foam – already a stronger wave had wet the silk fringes of this coat. I picked it up to move it away, its material was soft and light. It was a woman's coat.'

The process of discovery first that the pelisse was charming, then that the fringe was silk, then that the garment was a woman's is not nature but art. The woman, Elisa Schlésinger, was real enough, but her rising from the sea to dazzle an innocent boy has more to do with Venus Anadyomene than with any actual bourgeoise who went on holiday in 1836. Flaubert wants us to think that he happened upon the bathing spot innocently and 'par hasard' but he certainly knew where the bathing place was, because he had swum there with his family two summers before. On his return from Trouville in 1834, still six months shy of his thirteenth birthday, he wrote to Chevalier, his elder by a year:

We went for a dip in the sea several times over three days. One of the other people bathing was a lady, oh, a pretty lady, innocent although married, pure although she was twenty-two. Oh, how beautiful she was with her pretty blue eyes! The day before, we saw her laughing on the beach as her husband read to her, and the following day... we learnt... that she had been drowned yes, drowned, dear Ernest, in less than quarter of an hour the wave had swept her away... her husband who had stayed behind on the beach to watch her bathing saw her disappear.

He speaks of the young woman to his friend as if he were already a disillusioned roué, tacitly disparaging both marriage and women's virtue. The lifelong pose was already taken. He does not tell this story in *Memoirs of a Madman*; instead we are told of a dream in which he is walking by a river with his mother who suddenly falls into the water; he sees the water bubble up and ripples spread, but she does not resurface. He hears her calling, but when he throws himself down and peers into the water, he can see nothing: 'The water flowed on, flowed limpidly on, and that voice I could hear from the depths of the river plunged me into despair and rage...'

It is only to be expected that a child on the brink of his teens should recycle the tragic death of a young wife as a nightmare with himself in the position of the helpless husband. In *Memoirs of a Madman*, he elaborates the motif of the male on dry land and the female in the water. Although he went every day to watch his Venus bathe, he never thought of getting closer to her by becoming a bather himself. He remains in the position of the helpless husband, but this time the subject of his gaze does not disappear. Though the water can hardly have been as limpid as that of his dream-river, he can see Maria, as he calls her, 'de loin', from a distance, immersed in the water, and envies the wavelet 'lapping against her sides and covering with foam that heaving breast.' There is no need to unpack this description of its sexual content, because the erotic sequence is knowingly contrived. If the researchers who hunted down the real-life original of Maria had tried to watch swimmers 'de loin' they would have realised at once that what Flaubert claims to have seen cannot be seen. The sexual stimuli that shower from Maria, her exotic appearance, her scent, the burning heat of her flesh, her engorged breast, her voice, her foam-flecked panting bosom, all are imagined. The climax, an idyllic boat-trip by night, is pure E.T.A. Hoffmann. The vividness of the constructed fantasies is the best evidence that the boy did spend a sleepless night watching his bedside candle burning down and torturing himself with imagining his goddess and her 'vulgar and jovial' husband making love. And there are no prizes for identifying the melting candle with the post-masturbatory penis. Though Madame Schlésinger was a real person, the Maria of *Memoirs of a Madman* is an imaginary construct to which Flaubert would return again and again.

At eighteen, Flaubert did go swimming in the sea off Marseilles; this time his wet body caught the eye of a beautiful thirty-five-year-old woman who came to his hotel room and introduced him to 'an orgy of delights' which left him detumescent, miserable and utterly disgusted with himself and her. Like Maria she was dark, with the same aquiline nose and features *à l'antique*, with even the same dark down on her upper lip. For six months after their encounter, Flaubert, who had no interest in seeing the woman again, made love to her by letter. The pleasure was not in the sex but in writing about it.

Seduced by the cunning of the telling, commentators have allowed themselves to take at face value Flaubert's claims that Madame Schlésinger was his only love. In fact the distant, unattainable, fleshly goddess has been the only successful love object since the beginning of literature, which is about neither cohabitation nor copulation, but courtship. A woman enjoyed is a goddess destroyed. Flaubert liked to say that Lesbos was his native land; he could have learnt the imagery of unslaked desire from Sappho who described it six centuries before the birth of Christ or, closer to home, in medieval Provençal lyrics. In following the creed that (in Keats' words) 'Heard memories are sweet, but those unheard are sweeter', Flaubert is simply romantic. What has changed for him and contemporaries like Baudelaire, the De Goncourt brothers, Daudet, and De Maupassant, is that they put the notion to the test by exploring physical, even criminal pleasures, and minutely recording their disgust. Even in this, they followed in the footsteps of Ovid, Martial, Petronius and Juvenal. Flaubert's narrator/hero is the lineal descendant of a long line of despairing young men, of the speaker of Rochester's 'Satire upon Reason and Mankind', say, or Byron's *Childe Harold* or Goethe's *Werther*; he is also the forebear of the narrator of Sartre's *Nausea*. In his dreamy love idealism, his fastidious rejection of the everyday, and his desperate unhappiness, he is also Emma Bovary.

As Flaubert says, everyone would rather be a madman than a fool. Every day young men set up 'madman' personal websites on the internet where other madmen may visit them and swap rants against conformism, bourgeois society and pop culture. There are diaries of madmen on video, film and vinyl. Their disgust, like the disgust that Flaubert cultivated from his childhood, is an artefact. Flaubert lived his revulsion; he elaborated it into the habit of mind that we now call 'bovarism' and wrote a sublime novel about its female victim. The pose is still compelling; most of the young people who adopt it will abandon it, accept bourgeoisification and join the consumer culture. For those who don't – few or none of whom will have Flaubert's obsessive devotion to his craft – misery, ill-health and ultimate self-destruction are more likely outcomes than the creation of a masterpiece.

– Germaine Greer, 2002

'FLAUBERT: Spent days labouring over a single sentence. – But some say his works lack vitality. – Don't forget to mention *Flaubertian irony*, with a knowing look.'

For most of his life as a writer, Flaubert collected materials for a *sottisier*, a book of remarks, culled from his reading and things overheard in everyday life, that he thought distinguished by their incorrectness, platitude, or stupidity. Many of these ended up in the *Dictionary of Received Ideas* that he planned to append to his last, unfinished novel, *Bouvard and Pécuchet,* as a grotesque sample of the clichés and commonplaces to which all the world's wisdom was degraded in the mouths of the bourgeoisie of nineteenth-century France. The above is an imaginary entry on Flaubert himself: the three components of stylistic perfection, a perhaps deficient or frozen sensibility, and an irony all the more unremitting for being finally undecidable, are all part of the legend of Flaubert as it was already developing in his own time and as it has not really changed a great deal since. But the reader aware of the legend, or coming to the two short pieces in this volume after encountering the Flaubert of *Madame Bovary* or *Sentimental Education*, is in for a surprise. The immaculate stylist here seems capable of producing work distinguished by diffuseness, repetition, and odd errors of fact (he thinks a pug-dog has a thick white coat). The Flaubert who would be capable of calculating with millimetric precision the position of a comma here shows a refreshing disregard for the elementary rules of punctuation (breathless strings of nouns, as when the protagonist of the *Memoirs of a Madman* claims to have loved 'chariots horses uniforms of war the beat of the drums...'). The Flaubert whose subtle handling of tenses was one of the reasons for which he was hailed by Proust as renovating our perception of the world in the same way as Kant's categories here slips casually and confusingly from tense to tense with no apparent rationale, and at times produces sentences that are pleasantly ungrammatical. Where his main work is rigorously in the third person, and notoriously impersonal in tone, here we have a first-person narrative (the *Memoirs*) that seems at times uncomfortably close to autobiography: it launches into metaphysical speculation, expresses opinions on everything under the sun (and several things over it), and indulges in a direct and at times emotional lyricism, while any irony is confined to a recognition of the fact that it is an adolescent who is talking, and all adolescents feel this way (while also being convinced that they are alone in their mood swings between idealistic élan and nihilistic *taedium vitae*) – for the narrator acknowledges that even at his most intensely world-weary, he cannot avoid striking a pose common to all the other cynical and romantic young men of nineteenth-century France.

The reader who finds the result un-Flaubertian in its inelegance and, at times, its opacity, can lay part of the blame at the feet of the translator. But there is something appealingly spontaneous and, for all the romantic clichés, exploratory about the writing – and in any case, Flaubert had an excuse that the translator does not: when he wrote the *Memoirs* and 'Bibliomania', he was still in his mid teens. These are both 'oeuvres de jeunesse', and have to be read as such, for while Flaubert started writing young, he was not otherwise precocious in terms of talent or achievement. In these early works, Flaubert was as yet far removed from the heroically dedicated seeker after *le mot juste* he was to become: *Memoirs of a Madman* was not even published in his lifetime, and shows several traces of incompleteness, while 'Bibliomania', his first published work, although quite effective as a piece of storytelling, is a world away from the narrative and descriptive scruples of the major novels or even, for all their (perfectly contrived) air of innocence, the late *Three Tales*. And yet if in one sense his mature work (from *Madame Bovary* onwards) was to be a rejection of all that is stylistically unrefined in these early pieces, the themes they handle were to preoccupy him throughout his career. *Memoirs*, in particular, is a compendium of material that he was to rework ceaselessly – verbose but swarming with inchoate life, it is the primordial soup from which the mature writer was to crawl laboriously onto dry land.

One aspect of the *Memoirs* that was to persist in Flaubert's *oeuvre* is its visionary quality. Its adolescent hero is prone to cosmic fantasies of an intensity that goes some way beyond those of most teenagers. (It is unsure to what extent the hero really *is* adolescent – the text, with its circularity, its anticipations of what life will be like, its premonitions of how the protagonist will feel when he is the old man he already half seems to be and looks back on a life lived largely in the imagination, creates the sense of a chronological haze bordering on complete incoherence, or perhaps simply reports perfectly accurately the strangely timeless stasis, the sense of an anachronistic self without narrative bearings or forward momentum, that afflicts adolescents, and some artists, in particular). If there is a madness in the text, it lies in these visions – periods from the historical past are hallucinated in impressionistic but compelling intensity, and the narrator's imaginings spin round in metaphysical vortices and apocalyptic fantasies of a prophetic, vengeful quality. Flaubert rings the changes on the ambivalent status of madness – boon and bane, privilege and curse, the mark of the solitary, alienated, singular being removed almost entirely from human communication (not only is this adolescent seen to be a misanthropic daydreamer by his fellows, but the disjunction between the words he shares with them and the particular things and emotions he is striving to express is a leitmotif of the work) and yet the most universal of characteristics (is the narrator's soul his own, or someone else's, he asks; he talks of the world itself as a howling, slobbering madman; and all language risks being in demented excess of an unknowable reality). Still, it is hard to see him as really mad.

Flaubert's story was contemporary with Nikolai Gogol's similarly-titled 'Diary [or Notes – *Zapiski*] of a Madman' (1834), and the romanticism of which the young Flaubert and Gogol were both in their idiosyncratic and dissident ways exemplars, paid eloquent homage to madness as not just an escape from but a critique of a world in which industrialisation and mechanisation seemed increasingly to privilege calculative rationality (or simply, for Flaubert, 'the bourgeois') above all else. But while Gogol's lonely, downtrodden clerk really does go mad (he imagines that he can hear dogs conversing, he obsessively speculates on the problems that will be caused when the earth lands on the moon, and finally decides that he is in fact the King of Spain), Flaubert's character is too lucid to do more than mimic the stereotypes of madness: however powerful the cosmic visions, they too often verge on the vacuous rather than the prophetic. But this is part of Flaubert's point, and one of the many ways in which the text anticipates his major works: given a world derelict of passion, glamour, or at times any significant meaning whatsoever, the *Memoirs* open up various escape routes which offer, if only for a moment, some transcendence. But each of them turns out to be a dead-end. Madness turns out to be no exit from the humdrum *Weltschmerz* of an unusually articulate but otherwise unremarkable teenager. Chapter 2 evokes childhood and its enticing dreams, only to reflect bitterly on the wasted hours spent mulling them over by the fireside. The hero recounts how his poetic musings gave way to what he calls 'meditation', in other words philosophy, only immediately to cast doubt on the value of endlessly dissecting hypotheses and setting out 'in geometrical style the emptiest words' (the reference to geometry may allude to Spinoza's *Ethics*, a work drawn up in Euclidean deductive style, and a lifelong inspiration to Flaubert – though one that he would again distance himself from in that encyclopedia of disenchantment, *Bouvard and Pécuchet*). Chapter 3 pits the narrator against his philistine schoolteachers and boorish schoolmates, and shows him escaping into dreams of fame, travel (especially to the East), and history (especially that of the Middle Ages and the ancient world), all themes to which the author would repeatedly return – travelling to the Orient in his late twenties; ceaselessly writing and revising his *Temptation of Saint Anthony*, that visionary, phantasmagoric catalogue of the sensual allurements and heresies besetting the hermit Anthony of Egypt (251–356 CE); composing *Salammbô*, his account of ancient Carthage shortly after the First Punic War; and depicting in the *Three Tales* both the medieval Saint Julian the Hospitaller, and Palestine at the time of the execution of John the Baptist. Some readers have found the disjunction between this wide range of reference and the apparent narrowness of sensibility disconcerting: all those saints (Anthony, Julian, John) and so little real transcendence; all those encounters with otherness both geographical and historical, and so little sense of a real dynamic interplay between self and other. This is an unnecessarily negative appraisal of Flaubert's career – but it is one that his narrator in the *Memoirs* seems to anticipate. His metaphysical and religious speculations are so intense as to induce vertigo in him, but they constantly relapse into a yawn accompanied by a shrug. The fate of all dreams of knowledge is scepticism, and transcendence, even through art, is withheld. With one partial exception. Love is the mode of attempted transcendence that the *Memoirs* treat most seriously, and it is here that the autobiographical reference is most specific: the narrator's encounter with 'Maria' is a variation on the fourteen-year-old Flaubert's calf love for the twenty-five-year-old Elisa Schlésinger, whom he met at Trouville: she was to be fictionalised into the shadowy, unknowable Madame Arnoux, love-object of Frédéric Moreau in *Sentimental Education*, demure yet tantalising, perfectly ordinary but ardently longed for, maternal but distant. This first love makes Frédéric's later affairs 'insipid', and a similar claim has been made about the paralysing effect on Flaubert of his youthful infatuation for Elisa/'Maria' (the hero's flirtation with Caroline, in the *Memoirs*, seems designed to show precisely how little any other woman will mean to him in comparison with Maria). But this love at least survives the corrosive nihilism that undermines so many of the other values the text entertains. If nihilism is, as so often in Flaubert, the response to the realisation that human beings cannot have it all, cannot encompass – as his Faustian dreams desired – *the* All (Flaubert was reading Goethe's *Faust* just before his fateful holiday in Trouville), the text holds out, against the vague immensities of sea and sky, the cosmic longing to range through all of space and time, and the adolescent all-or-nothing apocalypticism, *minute particulars* – the Italian tune Maria hums as she breast-feeds her child, her white foot with its pink toenails sinking into the sand, her husband's ability to walk three leagues to get a decent melon. Love for Maria, even if 'unrealised', makes the narrator what so far in the *Memoirs* he has not been: a potential realist novelist, someone capable of love of the real *as realised in language* (even if the reality that is the pretext of that language can at times be infuriatingly obtuse or withdrawn). Maria, however constructed, is the birth of realism.

'Bibliomania' is a short fable whose kernel Flaubert took from a (probably fictitious) newspaper story. Its hero, Giacomo, is a passionate book-collector: the fact that he is barely able to read makes of him a Borgesian blind librarian *avant la lettre*. And as in Borges the story is suffused with paranoia and a sense of malediction: an obsessive devotion to books can be murderous, as the mysterious epidemic of deaths in Barcelona that seems particularly to afflict bibliophiles suggests. Giacomo is a hoarder of words, of curios and rarities and cultural riches that in their objectified, commodified form add up to no significant meaning for him. He is put on trial by a suspicious society that scapegoats eccentric solitaries like him, and he dies because of his refusal to accept that the prized possession for which he has risked his life is not in fact the only copy in Spain. The fifteen-year-old Flaubert, who years later would be brought before the courts for the 'immoral' book he had sacrificed himself to, the laboriously composed *Madame Bovary*, and who was haunted all life long by the fear that what we think of as most unique may in fact be just one of many copies, has here written a strangely prophetic tale.

– Andrew Brown, 2002

Note on Publication Dates:
Memoirs of a Madman (*Les Mémoires d'un fou*) was written for Flaubert's friend, Alfred Le Poittevin, in 1838. It was serialised in four parts in *La Revue blanche* from December 1900 to February 1901, and also published as a single volume in 1901. 'Bibliomania' ('Bibliomanie') was Flaubert's first work to be printed, in *Le Colibri*, a Rouen review, in February 1837. Both works are here translated from the 'Pléiade' edition of the *Oeuvres de jeunesse* (*Oeuvres complètes*, vol. I), edited by Claudine Gothot-Mersch and Guy Sagnes (Paris: Gallimard, 2001).

Memoirs of a Madman

At this time of year when we usually give and receive presents, we exchange gold and handshakes. – But I am giving you my thoughts; a poor present! Accept them – they are yours, as is my heart.

– *Gustave Flaubert, 4th January 1839*

To you my dear Alfred these pages are dedicated as a gift.

They contain an entire soul – is it mine, is it someone else's? I had at first wished to write an intimate novel in which scepticism would be driven to the final limits of despair, but little by little as I wrote, my personal impressions broke through the fable, my soul gripped my quill and flattened its tip.

So I prefer to leave it in the mystery of conjecture – you, I know, will conjecture nothing.

But you will perhaps think that the expression in several places is forced and the picture darkened just for the fun of it. Remember that it is a madman who wrote these pages, and if the words often seem in excess of the feelings they express it is because, in other places, they have sagged beneath the weight of emotion.

*

Farewell, think of me and for me.

1

Why write these pages? – What are they good for? – What do I myself know about it? It is foolish enough in my view to go round asking people the reason for their actions and the things they write. – Do you yourself know why you have opened the wretched pages that the hand of a madman is going to write?

A madman. That inspires horror. And what are you, reader? in which category do you place yourself, in that of fools or that of the mad? If you were given the choice, your vanity would still incline you to the latter condition. Yes, once again, what is it good for, I ask in all truth, a book that is neither instructive nor amusing, neither chemical nor philosophical nor agricultural nor elegiac, a book that gives no recipes for mutton or for getting rid of fleas, that talks neither of railways nor of the Stock Exchange nor of the intimate recesses of the human heart nor of medieval costume, neither of God nor of the Devil, but which talks about a madman, by which I mean the world, that great idiot that has been rotating for so many centuries in space without moving forward a single step, and that howls and slobbers and tears itself apart.

I don't know any more than you what you are about to read. For this is not a novel or a drama with a fixed plan, nor a single premeditated idea, with perfectly straight alleys staked out, down which your thoughts can meander.

But I am going to put down on paper everything that springs to mind, my ideas with my memories, my impressions my dreams my whims, everything which passes through my thoughts and my soul – laughter and tears, white and black, sobs that well up in the heart and are then rolled out like pastry in sonorous periods; – and tears diluted in romantic metaphors. And yet it oppresses me to think that I'll be flattening the tips of a whole packet of pens, that I'll be using up a bottle of ink, that I'll be boring the reader and boring myself. I have become so accustomed to laughter and scepticism that the reader will find it's one perpetual joke from beginning to end; and the merry folk who enjoy a good laugh will by the end be able to laugh at the author and at themselves.

You will see how necessary it is to believe in a plan governing the universe, in the moral duties of mankind, in virtue and in philanthropy – a word that I feel like writing on my boots, when I get some, so that everyone can read it and learn it by heart, even the most short-sighted of them, the smallest, creepiest and crawliest of creatures, those closest to the gutter.

It would be wrong to see in this anything other than the recreations of a madman. A madman!

And you, reader – perhaps you have just got married or paid off your debts?

2

So I am going to write the story of my life – what a life! But have I lived? I am young, my face is without a wrinkle – and my heart without passion. – Oh! how calm life was, how mild and happy it appears, tranquil and pure! Oh! yes, peaceful and silent like a tomb in which the soul is the corpse.

I have barely lived: I have not known the world – that is, I have no mistresses, no flatterers, no servants, no baggage – I have not, as they say, gone into society, as it has always appeared to me false and loud and wreathed in tinsel, boring and stuck-up.

But life is not a series of deeds. My life is my thoughts.

So what is this thought that now leads me, at the age when everyone smiles and decides they are happy, when they get married, when they fall in love, at the age when so many others are intoxicated by all the love affairs and all the celebrity, when so many lights glitter and the glasses at the feast are full, to find myself solitary and naked, cold to all inspiration and all poetry, feeling that I'm dying and laughing cruelly at my prolonged death throes like that Epicurean who had his veins opened, bathed himself in perfume and died laughing like a man emerging drunk from an orgy that has worn him out.

Oh! how long it lasted, that thought! Like a hydra it devoured me with all its many mouths.

The thought of loss and bitterness, the thought of a weeping jester, the thought of a meditating philosopher...

Oh! yes, how many hours have slipped by in my life, long and monotonous, as I thought and doubted! How many winter days have I spent with my head lowered, in front of embers whitened by the pale reflection of the setting sun; how many summer evenings out in the fields at dusk watching the clouds fleeing and unfurling, the wheat fields waving in the breeze, hearing the woods rustling and listening to nature sighing at night.

Oh! how dreamy was my childhood, what a poor madman I was, without fixed ideas, without positive opinions! I would watch the water flow between the clumps of trees dangling their leaves like a head of hair and dropping their blossom; I would contemplate from my cradle the moon

7

shining in the dark blue sky lighting up my bedroom and drawing strange shapes on the walls; I would fall into ecstasy at the sight of beautiful sunlight or a spring morning with its white mist, its blossoming trees, its daisies in flower.

I also liked, and this is one of my tenderest and most delightful memories, to watch the sea, the waves foaming over each other, the swell breaking into spray, sweeping right across the beach and crying aloud as it withdrew over the pebbles and sea shells.

I would run from rock to rock, taking the sand of the ocean and letting it drift in the wind as it trickled through my fingers, I would splash the seaweed, I would breathe in deep that fresh salty ocean air that infuses your soul with such energy, with poetic and far-reaching thoughts.

I looked out at the immensity, space, the infinite, and my soul was swallowed up before this limitless horizon.

Oh! but that is not where the limitless horizon really is! The vast abyss. Oh! no, a wider and deeper abyss opened up before me. That abyss is untroubled by any storm: if it could be stormy, it would be full – and it is empty!

I was cheerful and happy, loving life and my mother, poor mother!

I still remember my little joys as I watched the horses racing down the road, saw the smoke of their breath and the sweat soaking their harnesses; I loved their monotonous and rhythmic trot, jogging the main braces; and then when we stopped – all was quiet in the fields. You could see the smoke billowing from their nostrils, the carriage rocked and then settled back on its springs, the wind blew against the windows, and that was all...

Oh! how wide I opened my eyes too at the sight of the crowd in holiday clothes, merry, with its tumultuous cries, a stormy sea of men, even more bad-tempered than the tempest and more stupid than its fury.

I loved chariots horses armies uniforms of war the beat of the drums, the noise the gunpowder and the cannons rolling over the cobbled streets of the towns.

As a child I loved what can be seen, as a teenager what can be felt, as a man I no longer love anything. And yet how many things I have in my soul, how much inner strength and how many oceans of anger and love crash together and break in this heart so weak, so feeble so fallen so weary so exhausted!

I am told I should once more get out into life, mix with the crowd!... but how can the broken branch bear fruit, how can the leaf torn away by the winds and dragged through the dust grow green again? and why, so young, such bitterness? What do I know? It was perhaps my destiny to live like this, weary before having borne any burden, out of breath before having run...

I have read, I have worked filled with the ardour of enthusiasm... I have written... Oh! how happy I was then, how high my thought in its delirium flew up into those regions unknown to man, where there is neither world nor planets nor suns! I had an infinity even more immense if that is possible than the infinity of God, in which poetry floated and stretched out its wings in an atmosphere of love and ecstasy, and then I had to descend from those sublime regions to words, and how can one translate into words that harmony which arises in the poet's soul, and the giant thoughts which make the sentences bend and bow as a strong swollen hand splits open the glove wrapped round it?

There too lay disappointment, for we come back to earth, to that earth[1] of ice where all fire dies, where all energy drains away. By what rungs can one descend from the infinite to the positive? By what stages can thought lower itself without breaking apart? How can one cut down to size that giant who embraces the infinite?

Then I had moments of gloom and despondency, I felt my strength breaking me and that weakness I was ashamed of – for words are but the distant, muffled echo of thought. I cursed my dearest dreams and my silent hours spent on the limits of creation. I felt something empty and insatiable devouring me.

Tired of poetry, I launched myself into the field of meditation.

At first I fell in love with that imposing study which takes man as its subject and sets out to explain him, going so far as to dissect hypotheses and argue over the most abstract suppositions and to set out in geometrical style the emptiest of words.

Man, a grain of sand thrown into the infinite by an unknown hand, a poor insect with feeble little legs trying at the edge of the abyss to keep its grip on every branch, holding on tight to virtue, love, egoism, ambition, and turning all these things into virtues so as better to hang on, clinging to God and yet still weakening, letting go and falling...

Man, who wants to understand what is not, and develop a science of nothingness; man, a soul made in God's image and whose sublime genius is arrested by a blade of grass and cannot overcome the problem of a speck of dust.

And weariness overcame me, I began to doubt everything. Though young I was old, my heart was wrinkled and seeing old men still full of life, of enthusiasm and beliefs, I would laugh bitterly at myself, so young, so disabused of life, of love, of fame, of God, of all that is, of all that can be. However, I was seized by a natural horror before embracing this faith in nothingness. At the edge of the abyss I closed my eyes – I fell in.

I was happy, I no longer had any further to fall, I was cold and calm like a tombstone – I thought I could find happiness in doubt, crazy as I was! You spin through it as through an incommensurable void.

That void is immense and makes your hair stand up in horror when you draw near its edge.

From doubting God I finally came to doubting virtue, that fragile idea which each century has set up to the best of its ability on an even shakier scaffolding of laws.

I will tell you later all the phases of this gloomy and meditative life spent by the fireside with my arms folded, with an eternal yawn of boredom – alone for a whole day – and turning from time to time to look at the snow on the neighbouring rooftops, the sunset with its pale light spilling across the flagstones of my bedroom, or a yellow death's head with its fixed toothless grimace on my mantelpiece, a symbol of life and, like life, cold and mocking.

Later on you will perhaps read of all the anguishes of this heart so battered, so broken with bitterness. You will learn about the adventures of this life, so peaceful and so commonplace, so full of emotions, so empty of events.

And then you will tell me if it is not all derision and mockery, if everything sung in the schools, all the nonsense spun out in books, everything that can be seen felt and said, everything that exists…

I can't finish, my bitterness is too great to express it – oh! if only all this were not in the end to be mere pity, smoke, nothingness!

3

I went to school as soon as I was ten and there I developed early on a profound aversion for men – the society of children is as cruel towards its victims as that other little society – that of men. –

The same injustice of the crowd, the same tyranny of prejudice and force, the same egoism, however much people talked about the disinterestedness and loyalty of youth. Youth – the age of madness and dreams, of poetry and folly, those synonyms in the mouths of people who judge the world *soundly*. There I was rebuffed in all my tastes – in class for my ideas, during break for my tendencies towards a savage unsociability.

From then on I was a madman.

So I lived there alone and bored, harassed by my masters and jeered at by my schoolmates. I had a mocking and independent temperament, and my biting and cynical irony was no more sparing of an individual whim than it was of the despotism of them all.

I can still see myself on the classroom benches, absorbed in my dreams of the future, thinking of the most sublime things which the imagination of a poet and a child can dream up, while the teacher made fun of my Latin verse, and my schoolmates sniggered at me. The idiots, them laughing at me! when they were so feeble, so common, so narrow-minded – whereas I, whose spirit was immersed in the limits of creation, who was absorbed in all the worlds of poetry, I who felt myself to be greater than them all, was granted infinite pleasures and experienced heavenly raptures at all the intimate revelations of my soul.

I, who felt myself as vast as the world and whom a single one of my thoughts, if it had been of fire like a bolt of lightning, could have reduced to dust. Poor madman!

I could see myself young, at twenty, wreathed in glory, I would dream of long voyages into the countries of the South, I could see the Orient and its vast sands, its palaces through which roamed camels with little bronze bells, I could see mares dashing off towards the horizon bathed in red sunlight, I could see blue waves, a pure sky, silver sand, I could smell the fragrance of those warm oceans of the South, and then near me, beneath a tent in the shade of a broad-leaved aloe tree, a woman with brown skin and an ardent gaze, who enfolded me in her arms and spoke to me in the language of houris[2].

The sun was sinking into the sand, the she-camels and the mares were asleep, insects buzzed round their dugs, the evening breeze blew close by – and when night had fallen, as the silver moon gazed palely down onto the desert, and the stars shone out in that dark blue sky, then in the silence of that warm and fragrant night, I would dream of infinite joys, and pleasures which are those of heaven.

And then again it was fame with its applause, its fanfares rising skywards, its laurel wreaths, its gold dust strewn in the winds – it was a brilliant theatre with women in all their finery, diamonds with all their glitter, a heavy atmosphere, panting bosoms – then a religious sense of absorption, words as all-devouring as a fire, tears, laughter, sobs, the intoxication of fame – exclamations of enthusiasm, the crowd stamping its approval. What! – vanity, noise, nothingness.

As a child I dreamt of love – as a young man of fame – as a man, of the tomb, that last love of those who have no love left.

I could also descry the ancient period of vanished centuries and of races laid to rest under the grass, I could see the band of pilgrims and warriors marching towards Calvary, stopping in the desert, dying of starvation, imploring the same God they were on their way to seek, and weary of their blasphemies continuing to march towards that endless horizon – then, exhausted, panting, finally reaching their journey's end, despairing and aged, to embrace a few arid stones to which the entire world paid homage; – I could see iron-clad knights riding on iron-clad horses, and lances clashing in the tournaments, and the drawbridge being lowered to receive the suzerain returning with his sword running red and captives on the crupper of his horses; or at night in the dark cathedral, the whole nave adorned with a garland of nations rising up towards the vault in the galleries, with songs, lights glowing resplendent on the stained-glass windows, and, on the night of Christmas, the old city with its pointed snow-covered rooftops, all lit up and singing. –

But it was Rome I loved – imperial Rome, that beautiful queen wallowing in orgies, spattering her noble robes with the wine of debauchery, prouder of her vices than she was of her virtues. – Nero – Nero with his diamond chariots flying into the arena, his thousand carriages, his tigerish loves and his giant feasts. – Far from lessons in the classics I would take myself back to your immense pleasures, your blood-drenched illuminations, your amusements that set Rome on fire.

And lulled by these vague reveries, these hazy dreams of the future, carried away by that venturesome imagination roaming like an unbridled mare fording torrents, galloping up mountainsides and flying off into space – I would spend hours at a time with my head in my hands gazing at the floor of my study or at a spider weaving its web on our master's lectern – and when I came to, dazed and wide-eyed, they all laughed at me – the laziest boy in the class, who would never have a single positive idea, who showed no inclination for any profession, who would be useless in this world where everyone has to go off and get their slice of the cake, and who would ultimately never be good for anything, at best merely a jester, a keeper of fairground animals, or a maker of books.

(Although in excellent health, my type of mind, permanently set on edge by the life I was leading and by contact with others, had caused me to develop a nervous irritability which made me abrasive and quick-tempered like the bull driven mad by insect stings. – I had dreams, dreadful nightmares.)

Oh! a sad and cheerless time! I can still see myself wandering alone down the long whitewashed corridors of my school, looking, looking at the owls and the crows taking flight from the gables of the chapel; or else, in bed in those gloomy dormitories lit by the lamp in which the oil froze at night, I would listen for hours to the wind blowing lugubriously in the long empty apartments and whistling through the keyholes as it rattled the windows in their frames, I could hear the footsteps of the night-watchman slowly doing his rounds with his lantern and when he came close to me I pretended to be asleep, and I would indeed doze off, half in dreams and half in tears.

4

They were fearful visions, enough to drive you mad with terror.

I was in bed in my father's house, all the furniture had been preserved, and yet everything surrounding me had a black hue; it was a winter night and the snow was shedding a white gleam into my bedroom – suddenly the snow melted and the trees and the grass took on a reddish-brown, burnt tint as if a fire had been casting its glow on my windows. I could hear footsteps – someone was coming upstairs – a warm gust of air, a fetid vapour rose up to me – my door opened by itself. They came in, there were a lot of them – perhaps seven or eight, I didn't have the time to count them. They were short or tall, black-bearded ruffians – without weapons, but all with a steel blade between their teeth, and, as they encircled my cradle, their teeth started chattering and it was horrible; they drew aside my white curtains and every finger left a streak of blood; they gazed at me with great staring lidless eyes. I gazed at them too – I couldn't move a muscle – I wanted to scream.

It seemed to me then that the house was rising out of its foundations, as if prised up by a lever.

They gazed at me like this for quite a while, then they withdrew and I saw that all of them had one side of their faces flayed and slowly bleeding. –

They lifted up all my clothes and they were all blood-stained. – They began to eat and the bread they broke oozed blood which fell drop by drop; and they started to laugh, like the death rattle of a dying man.

Then when they were no longer there, everything they had touched, the panelling, the staircase, the ceiling, was all stained blood-red by them.

I had a taste of bitterness in my heart. I felt as if I had eaten flesh. And I heard a prolonged, raucous, sharp cry, and the windows and doors slowly swung open, and the wind made them slam and creak, like a strange song whose every shrill note drove a dagger through my breast.

Another time, there was verdant countryside scattered with flowers along a river; I was with my mother who was walking near the riverbank – she fell. – I saw the water foaming, the ripples widening and suddenly disappearing. – The stream resumed its course and then all I could hear was the sound of the water flowing between the rushes and bending the reeds.

All at once my mother called me: 'Help, help! oh my poor child, help me, help me!'

I flattened myself in the grass, leaning down to look, but I could see nothing; the cries continued. –

An invincible force was holding me fast – to the firm ground – and I could hear the cries: 'I'm drowning, I'm drowning, help me!'

The water flowed on, flowed limpidly on, and that voice I could hear from the depths of the river plunged me into despair and rage…

5

That, then, is what I was like – a carefree dreamer with an independent and mocking temperament, building up a destiny for myself and dreaming of all the poetry of a life filled with love; – and living on my memories, insofar as one can have many memories at sixteen.

I strongly disliked school. It would be an interesting subject to study, this profound disgust felt by noble and elevated souls, showing itself the minute they come into irksome contact with men. I have never liked a regular life, fixed hours, an existence ruled by the clock in which thought has to stop as soon as the bell rings, in which everything is wound up in advance for centuries and generations. This regularity may doubtless suit the majority, but for the poor child who draws nourishment from poetry, from dreams and fantasies, who thinks of love and every kind of nonsense, it means ceaselessly waking him out of this sublime dream, it means not leaving him a moment's peace, it means stifling him by dragging him back into our atmosphere of materialism and common sense, which inspire him with horror and disgust.

I would go off by myself with a book of verse, a novel – poetry, something to bring a thrill to the heart of a young man with as yet no experience of sensations and so very desirous of gaining some.

I recall with what intense pleasure I devoured, at that time, the pages of Byron, and of *Werther*, with what transports I read *Hamlet*, *Romeo*, and the most ardent productions of our age, all those works, in a word, that make the soul melt with rapture or set it aflame with enthusiasm.

So I drew sustenance from that rugged poetry of the

North which echoes so powerfully, like the waves of the sea, in the works of Byron. Often I could remember entire chunks after only one reading, and I would repeat them to myself like a song that has captivated you and whose melody continues to haunt you. How many times I recited the beginning of *The Giaour*: 'No breath of air'... or in *Childe Harold*: 'Whilome in Albion's isle' or 'And I have loved thee, Ocean!' The flatness of the French translation disappeared under the force of the ideas themselves as if they had had a style of their own without needing words as such.[3]

That fervent, passionate personality, imbued with such a deep sense of irony, could not fail to act strongly on an ardent, virginal nature. All those echoes, unknown to the sumptuous dignity of classical literature, had for me a fragrance of novelty, an allurement that made me return repeatedly to that gigantic poetry that gives you vertigo and makes you topple into the bottomless abyss of the infinite.

In this way I had corrupted my taste and my heart, as my teachers put it, and among so many beings of degraded proclivities, my independence of mind had resulted in the fact that I was considered the most depraved of all, reduced to the lowest level by my very superiority. They could barely bring themselves to concede that I did have imagination, that is, in their opinion, an overexcited brain that brought me to the verge of madness.

Such was my entry into society, and the esteem I earned there.

6

If my mind and my principles were denigrated, nobody attacked my heart, for I was kind in those days and another's misfortunes would move me to tears.

I remember that while still a child I liked to empty my pockets into those of the poor; I remember the smile with which they would greet me as I came by and the pleasure I took in doing them good. It is a pleasure that I have not experienced for a long time – for now I have a hard heart, my tears have dried up. But woe to the men who have made me corrupt and savage, when once I was kind and pure! Woe to that aridity of civilisation that parches and withers everything that grows in the sunshine of poetry and the glow of the heart! That old corrupt society which has been so seductive and so crafty, that old grasping Jew will die from emaciation and exhaustion on those heaps of manure he calls his treasures, without a poet to sing of his death, without a priest to close his eyes, without gold for his mausoleum, for he will have squandered it all on his vices.

7

So when will this society end, debased as it is by every debauchery, debauchery of mind, body, and soul?

Then, doubtless, there will be joy on earth, for that lying and hypocritical vampire called civilisation will finally die. Men will leave behind them the royal mantle, the sceptre, the diamonds, the tottering palace, the collapsing town, and go off to join the mare and the she-wolf. After having spent his life in palaces and worn out his feet on the flagstones of great cities, man will go off to die in the woods.

The earth will be parched by the fires that have burnt it, and filled with the dust of battles, the wind of desolation that has swept over man will have swept over it too, and it will henceforth bring forth only bitter fruit, and thorny roses.

And whole races will die out in the cradle like plants battered by the winds and dying before they have flowered.

For everything must have an end and the earth be worn down under the tramping of feet. For immensity must ultimately be weary of that speck of dust that makes so much noise and disturbs the majesty of nothingness. Gold will inevitably run out at last, having passed through men's hands and corrupted them. This haze of blood must subside, the palace must collapse under the weight of the riches it conceals, the orgy must finish and the time come to awaken.

Then there will be a huge peal of despairing laughter when men see this void, when they have to leave life for death – for all-devouring, ever-hungry death. And everything will break apart to collapse into nothingness – and the virtuous man will curse his virtue, and vice will clap its hands.

Some few men still wandering across an arid land will call out to each other, they will make their way towards one another, and they will recoil in horror, aghast at themselves, and die. What will man be then, he who is already fiercer than the wild beasts and more vile than the reptiles?

Farewell forever dazzling chariots, fanfares and glory, farewell to the world, to those palaces, to those mausoleums, to the delights of crime, and the joys of corruption; – the stone will fall suddenly crushed under its own weight and the grass will grow over it. – And the palaces, the temples, the pyramids, the columns, the king's mausoleums, the poor man's coffin, the dog's carcass, everything will be reduced to the same level under the grassy turf.

Then the sea no longer held back by walls will lap the shores in peace, and will bathe its waves on the still-smoking ashes of the cities, the trees will grow, leafy and green, without a hand to break and tear them, the rivers will flow through flowery meadows, nature will be free with no man to constrain her, and this race will be extinct for it was cursed from childhood. ...

... What a sad and strange period is ours, towards what ocean is this torrent of iniquities flowing? where are we going through a night so dark? – Those who want to palpate this sick world withdraw hurriedly, aghast at the corruption stirring restlessly in its entrails.

When Rome felt her death agony upon her she had at least one hope, she could see behind the shroud the radiant cross lighting up eternity. That religion has lasted for two thousand years and now it is exhausted, no longer adequate, an object of mockery; – see its churches falling, its cemeteries piled high with overflowing heaps of dead.

And as for us, what religion will we have?

To be as old as we are and to be still marching through the desert like the Hebrews fleeing from Egypt!

Where will be the Promised Land?

We tried everything and were starting to deny everything, devoid of hope – and then a strange greed seized us, there is an immense disquiet gnawing away at us, there is a sense of emptiness in our crowd. – We feel all around us a sepulchral chill in the soul; and humanity started to set machines in motion, and seeing the gold pouring from them it exclaimed: 'This is God!' – and that God it devours. There is...

– for all is over, farewell, farewell, some wine before we die!

Everyone rushes wherever his instincts impel him, the populace swarms like insects over a corpse, poets pass by without having the time to sculpt their thoughts, hardly have they scribbled their ideas down on sheets of paper than the sheets are blown away; everything glitters and everything resounds in this masquerade, beneath its ephemeral royalties and its cardboard sceptres, gold flows, wine cascades, cold debauchery lifts her skirts and jigs around... horror! horror! and then there hangs over it all a veil that each one grabs part of to hide himself the best he can.

Derision! Horror – horror!

8

And there are days when I feel an immense weariness, and a sombre boredom enwraps me like a shroud wherever I go, its folds hamper and constrain me, life weighs me down like remorse. So young and so weary when there are those who are old and still full of enthusiasm! And I who have fallen so far, and am so disenchanted – what am I to do? At night, to look at the moon that sheds its trembling gleam on my panelling like broad-leaved foliage, and in the daytime to look at the sun gilding the neighbouring roofs – is this a life? No, it is death but without the repose of the grave.

And I have little joys that belong to me alone, childish reminiscences which still come to warm me in my isolation like reflections from the setting sun through the bars of a prison. A trifle, the least circumstance, a rainy day, a bright sun, a flower, an old piece of furniture bring back to my mind a series of memories which all pass away, in disorder, disappearing like shadows. – Children's games on the grass in the midst of daisies in the meadows, behind the flowering hedge, alongside the vine with its golden bunches of grapes, on the brown and green moss, beneath the broad leaves, the fresh canopy of foliage. Calm and cheerful memories like a smile from earliest youth, you pass near me like withered roses.

Youth, its bubbling excitements, its confused instincts for the world and the heart, its tremulous love, its tears, its cries. The young man's love, the mature man's ironies. You often return with your dark or drab colours, fleeing along on each other's heels like the shades of the dead which rush by along the walls on winter nights; and I often fall into raptures at the memory of some pleasant day I spent long ago, a crazy day full of joy with moments of ebullience and laughter that still echo in my ears, a day that still vibrates with gaiety and makes me smile with bitterness. – It was a day I went horse riding, the horse leaping along and flecked with foam, or a time I went for a dreamy walk through a broad, shadowy garden path, watching the water flow over the pebbles, or else gazed at the sun dazzling and resplendent with its blaze of fire and its red halo, and

I can still hear the horse galloping, its nostrils smoking, I can hear the water rippling, the leaves rustling, the wind bending the wheat fields like the sea waves.

Others are gloomy and cold like rainy days, bitter, cruel memories which also come back to me – hours of torment spent hopelessly weeping, and then forcing laughter to chase away those tears which veil your eyes, those sobs which cover the sound of your voice. –

I spent many days, many years, sitting thinking of nothing, or of everything, plunged into the infinite that I wished to embrace, and that was devouring me.

I would hear the rain falling in the gutters, the bells tolling as I wept, I would see the sun slowly setting and night falling – the sleepy night that brings you peace; and then the day would return, always the same with its problems, the same number of hours to live, the day whose dying I watched with joy.

I would dream of the sea, of distant journeys, love affairs, triumphs, all the abortive things in my life, corpses before they had ever lived.

Alas! so none of that was meant for me. I do not envy others for everyone complains of the crushing burden that fate has imposed on him; – some throw it down before their life is over, others bear it to the end. And will *I* be able to bear it?

I have hardly seen life and there is already an immense disgust in my soul; I have brought to my lips every kind of fruit – they all seemed bitter to me, I thrust them away, and now I am dying of hunger. To die so young, without any hope in the tomb, without being sure that I will sleep there, without knowing whether its peace is inviolable – to throw yourself into the arms of nothingness and not to know whether it will receive you!

Yes I am dying, for is it living when you see your past as so much water that has flowed into the sea, when the present seems a cage, the future a shroud?

9

There are insignificant things which made a strong impression on me and which I will always keep like the imprint of a burning brand, although they are banal and silly.

I will always remember a kind of château not far from my town, which we often went to see. – It was one of those old women of the last century who lived there. Everything of hers had kept its pastoral feel – I can still see the powdered portraits, the sky-blue costumes of the men and the roses and the carnations scattered on the panelling with shepherdesses and flocks. – Everything had an old, sombre appearance, the furniture, almost all in embroidered silk, was spacious and comfortable – the house was ancient, surrounded by age-old ditches that at that time were planted with apple trees, and the stones that came away from time to time from the old battlements would go tumbling right down to the bottom.

Not far away was the park planted with great trees, with its dark paths, stone moss-covered benches, half broken-down, between the branches and the brambles. – A goat would be grazing and when you opened the iron gate, it would run off into the undergrowth.

On fine days the sunbeams would shine through the branches and gild the moss here and there. –

It was gloomy, the wind would blow into those wide

brick fireplaces and frighten me – especially in the evening when the owls would hoot in the vast lofts.

We would often prolong our visits until quite late in the evening, gathered round the old mistress in a big room whose floor was covered with white flagstones in front of a wide marble fireplace. I can still see her golden snuffbox full of the finest Spanish tobacco, her pug-dog with its long white coat, and her delicate little foot wrapped in a pretty high-heeled shoe decorated with a black rose.

*

How long ago all that was! The mistress is dead. Her pug-dogs too, her snuffbox is in the pocket of the notary – the château is used as a factory, and the poor shoe was thrown into the river.

*

AFTER THREE WEEKS' PAUSE:

… I am so weary that I find it too tedious to continue, having just reread the above.

Can the works of a bored man amuse the public?

And yet I am going to force myself to create better entertainment for both one and the other.

Here my Memoirs really begin…

10

Here are my tenderest and at the same time most painful memories, and I embark on them with a positively religious feeling. They are alive in my memory and still almost warm to my soul, since that passion made them bleed so much. It is a broad scar across my heart that will last forever, but as I recount this page of my life my heart is beating as if I were going to disturb some deeply cherished ruins. Those ruins are already old: as I have walked on through life, the horizon has receded behind me, and how many other things since then, for the days seem long, one by one from morning till evening! but the past seems swift so quickly does oblivion shrink the frame that contained it. For me everything still seems to be alive, I can hear and see the rustling of the leaves, I can see the slightest fold of her dress. – I can hear the timbre of her voice, as if an angel were singing near me.

A sweet, pure voice. – Which intoxicates you and makes you die with love. A voice so beautiful it has a body, and which seduces you as if there were a charm in your words...

It would be impossible for me to tell you the precise year. But at the time I was really young – I was, I think, fifteen; that year we went to the seaside resort of..., a village in Picardy, charming with its houses piled on top of one another, black, grey, red, white, facing every which way without alignment and without symmetry like a heap of shells and pebbles that the waves have thrown up onto the shore.

A few years ago no one ever went there despite its beach, a good half-league in length, and its charming position, but recently it has started to become fashionable; the last time I went there I saw a number of yellow-gloved dandies, and aristocratic liveries too; it was even being proposed to build a theatre there.

At that time everything was simple and remote, there was barely anyone except artists and locals. The shore was deserted, and at low tide you could see a huge beach with silvery grey sand glistening in the sun, still damp from the waves. – To the left, rocks where in its days of slumber the sea lapped lazily against the walls blackened with seaweed, then in the distance the blue ocean beneath a burning sun, roaring in muffled tones, like a weeping giant.

And when you returned to the village, it was the most picturesque and heart-warming spectacle: black nets corroded by the water hanging at the doors, everywhere half-naked children walking over the grey pebbles that were the only road surface in the whole place, sailors with their red and blue outfits, and the entire scene simple in its grace, innocent and hearty – all of it imbued with a character of vigour and energy.

I often went to walk along the shore by myself; one day chance had it that I walked in the direction of the area where people went swimming. It was a place not far from the last houses of the village, frequented more specifically for that purpose. – Men and women swam together; they undressed on the beach or in their houses and left their coats on the sand.

That day a charming red pelisse with black stripes had been left on the shore. The tide was rising – the shore was festooned with foam – already a stronger wave had wet the silk fringes of this coat. I picked it up to move it away, its material was soft and light. It was a woman's coat.

Apparently I had been seen, for that very day at lunch when everyone was eating in a common dining room at the inn where we were staying, I heard someone saying to me:

'Monsieur, thank you so much for your gallantry.'

I turned round.

It was a young woman sitting with her husband at the next table.

'What's that?' I asked, disconcerted.

'Thank you for picking up my coat: it was you, wasn't it?'

'Yes, Madame,' I replied in embarrassment.

She looked at me.

I lowered my gaze and blushed.

How she looked at me! – how beautiful this woman was! – I can still see those dazzling eyes beneath her black eyebrows gazing on me like a sun.

She was tall, dark, with magnificent black hair which fell in braids on her shoulders; her nose was Greek, her eyes burning, her eyebrows high and admirably arched; her skin was ardent and like velvet intermixed with gold, she was slender and fine-boned, you could see azure veins meandering down her brown and crimson neck. Add to that a fine down that shadowed her upper lip and gave her face a masculine and energetic expression enough to put blonde beauties in the shade. She might have been criticised for rather too full a figure, or instead for an artistic casualness – and women in general found her in vulgar; – she talked slowly, she had a modulated, musical, gentle voice. – She was wearing a fine dress of white muslin that showed off the soft outlines of her arms.

When she rose to leave, she put on a white bonnet with a single pink bow. She tied it with a delicate, dimpled hand, one of those hands you dream of for ages and that you long to cover with fiery kisses.

Every morning I would go to see her swimming, I gazed at her from afar beneath the water, I envied the soft peaceful waves lapping against her sides and covering with foam that heaving breast, I could see the outline of her limbs beneath the wet clothes enwrapping her, I could see her heart beating, her breast swelling, I mechanically contemplated her foot placing itself on the sand, and my gaze remained fixed to the trace of her steps and I could almost have wept at the sight of the waves slowly washing them away.

And then when she came back and passed by me, and I heard the water dripping from her clothes and the swish of her walk, my heart beat violently, I lowered my eyes, blood rushed to my head – I was suffocating – I could feel that woman's half-naked body passing by me with the odour of the waves. Even deaf and blind I would have guessed at her presence, for there was within me something intimate and tender which was submerged in ecstasy and graceful imaginings, whenever she passed by like that.

I still seem to see the place where I was rooted to the shore, I can see the waves sweeping in on every side, breaking and spreading out, I can see the beach festooned with foam, I can hear the sound of the mingled voices of the swimmers talking among themselves; I can hear her footsteps, I can hear her breath as she walked by me.

I was as motionless with stupor as if Venus had climbed down off her pedestal and started to walk. For this was the first time I was really aware of my heart, I could feel something mystical, strange, like a new sense. I was immersed in infinite, tender feelings, I was rocked by hazy, vague images, I had grown and at the same time become more proud.

I was in love.

To love: to feel young and full of love, to feel nature and its harmonies pulsating within you, to need that reverie, that activity of the heart, and to feel filled with happiness by it! Oh! a man's first heartbeats, his first throbbings of love, how sweet and strange they are! and later on, how silly and ridiculously stupid they seem!

The odd thing is that there is a mixture of torment and joy in that insomnia – is it the result once more of vanity?... Ah! could it be that love is merely pride? Must we deny what the most impious of people respect? Should we laugh – at the heart?

Alas! alas!

The wave has washed away Maria's footsteps.

It was at first a singular state of surprise and admiration; – a quite mystical sensation in some degree, all idea of pleasure excluded. It was only later that I felt that frenzied and sombre ardour of the flesh and the soul, an ardour that devours both of them.

I was in the astonishment of the heart experiencing its first throbs. I was like the first man when he had discovered all his faculties.

What did I dream of? it would be quite impossible to say – I felt myself new and all strange to myself, a voice had come into my soul; a trifle, a fold in her dress, a smile, her foot, the least meaningless word impressed themselves on me like supernatural things and I had enough to dream of for a whole day. I would follow her traces at the corner of a long wall and the rustle of her clothes made me quiver with pleasure.

When I heard her footsteps, the nights when she went for a walk or came towards me... no I cannot tell you how many sweet sensations of the heart's intoxication there are, how much of blessedness and folly there is in love.

And now that I am so full of mockery at everything, so bitterly convinced of the grotesque side of existence, I still have the feeling that love, the love I dreamt of at school without having it, and which I experienced later, which has made me weep so much and at which I have laughed so much, how firmly I still believe it can be at one and the same time the most sublime of things, or the most clownish of tomfooleries.

Two beings thrown into the world by chance, by something or other, and who happen to meet, fall in love because one is a woman and the other a man. – Look at them panting for each other, walking out together at night and getting damp with the dew, looking at the moonlight and finding it diaphanous, admiring the stars, and saying in every tone of voice: 'I love you you love me he loves me we love each other', and repeating it with sighs, with kisses – and then home they go, both impelled by an extraordinary ardour, for the organs of these two souls are violently overheating, and there they soon are grotesquely coupled roaring and sighing, both of them bent on reproducing another imbecile on earth, a wretch who will imitate them. Just look at them, more idiotic at this moment than dogs and flies, fainting away – and taking pains to hide from men's eyes their solitary pleasure, thinking perhaps that happiness is a crime and pleasure something shameful.

I will, I think, be forgiven for not talking about platonic love, that love exalted like that of a statue or a cathedral, that shuns any idea of jealousy and possession and which should be found shared mutually among men, but which I have rarely had occasion to observe. A sublime love if it existed, but which is only a dream like everything beautiful in this world.

I will stop here, for an old man's mockery should not tarnish the young man's virginal feelings; I would have been as indignant as you, reader, if I had had to hear such cruel language then.

I thought that a woman was an angel… Oh! how right Molière was to compare her to a bowl of soup![4]

11

Maria had a child – a little girl. – She was loved, hugged, fussed over with caresses and kisses. How happy I would have been to pick up a single one of those kisses shed like pearls, in profusion, on the head of that child in her swim-suit!

Maria was breast-feeding her herself – and one day I saw her opening her dress and presenting her breast to the child.

It was a plump round breast with brown skin and veins of deep blue visible beneath that ardent skin. Never had I seen a naked woman at that time. Oh! the singular ecstasy into which the sight of that breast plunged me – how I feasted my eyes on it, how I would have liked simply to touch that breast! It seemed to me that if I had placed my lips on it, my teeth would have bitten it in rage – and my heart melted with delight at the thought of the pleasures that kiss would give me.

Oh! I gazed at it repeatedly, for such a long time, that throbbing breast, that long graceful neck and that head bent down with its black hair in curl papers over her suckling child, as she rocked it gently on her knees, humming an Italian tune!

12

We soon got to know each other more intimately. – I say *we*, for can you imagine me personally plucking up courage to say anything to her, given the state the sight of her had put me in?

Her husband was something in between an artist and a commercial traveller. He was resplendent in moustaches and fashionable clothes – he smoked like a chimney, was lively – a good sort and amiable with it – not one to look down on the pleasures of the table: I once saw him walk three leagues for a melon from the next town. He had come with his post-chaise – with his dog, his wife, his child and twenty-five bottles of Rhenish wine.

At seaside resorts, in the countryside or while travelling, it is easier for people to talk – you want to get to know the others. – Any insignificant reason is enough for you to strike up a conversation; rain and shine take up even more time on these occasions than on others. People complain about their uncomfortable lodgings, and the horrors of inn food. These latter remarks especially show you have the best possible taste: 'Oh! the linen – so dirty! There's too much pepper, it's too spicy! Oh, how ghastly, my dear lady!'

If you go out walking together, everyone tries to outdo the others in their ecstatic outpourings over the beauty of the landscape. How lovely it is, how lovely the sea is! Add to this a few poetic and bombastic expressions, two or three philosophical observations interlarded with sighs and more or less heavy inhalations through the nose. If you can draw, then take out your morocco sketchbook – or, even better, pull your hat down over your eyes, fold your arms and go to sleep so as to give people the impression you are deep in thought.

There are women whose wit I have been able to sniff a quarter of a league off, simply by the way they were gazing at the waves.

And you must complain about men, eat little and wax passionate about a rock, admire a meadow and die of love for the sea. Ah! You will be exquisite – then everyone will say: 'The charming young man – what a nice smock he has, how elegant his boots are, what grace, what a beautiful soul!' It is this need to talk, this instinct for herding together in groups where the boldest march in front, which lies at the origin of societies and which these days brings together all social gatherings.

It was doubtless a similar reason that made us start talking for the first time. It was in the afternoon, it was warm and shafts of sunlight fell into the room in spite of the shutters. We had remained behind, a few painters, Maria, her husband and I, stretched out on chairs, smoking and drinking hot toddies.

Maria smoked, or at least if a remnant of feminine

stupidity prevented her from doing so, she liked the smell of tobacco (how monstrous!); she even gave me some cigarettes.

We talked about literature – an inexhaustible subject with women. – I participated fully; I spoke at length and with fiery enthusiasm; Maria and I were completely at one in our feelings about art. I have never known anyone with a more naive and less pretentious feel for it; she had a simple, expressive, striking way of putting things, and above all so much casual grace, so much unselfconsciousness, so much nonchalance – you would have said she was singing.

One evening her husband suggested we take a boat out. – The weather was the finest imaginable. We accepted.

13

How can one express in words those things for which there is no language, those impressions of the heart, those mysteries of the soul unknown to itself, how can I tell you of all that I felt, all that I thought, all the intense pleasures I experienced that evening?

It was a fine summer night; around nine o'clock we climbed into the rowing boat – the oars were put in place, we set off. – The weather was calm, the moon's reflection shone on the smooth surface of the water and the wake of the boat made its image waver under the ripples. The tide started to rise again and we felt the first waves slowly rocking the boat.

We were silent. Maria started talking. I do not know what she said, I yielded to the enchanting sound of her words as I yielded to the rocking of the sea. She was next to me, I could feel the outline of her shoulder and the contact of her dress, she was lifting her gaze towards the sky, pure, starry, resplendent with diamonds as it gazed down at its reflection in the blue waves.

She was an angel – when you saw her like that with her head raised and her celestial eyes.

I was heartsick with love; I could hear the two oars rising rhythmically, the waves beating the sides of the boat, I succumbed to the caressing touch of it all, as I listened to Maria's voice, gentle and vibrant.

Will I ever be able to describe to you all the melodies of her voice, all the grace of her smile, all the beauties of her gaze, will I ever succeed in telling you how it was enough to make me die of love, that night full of the fragrance of the sea with its transparent waves, its sand silvered by the moon – that fine, calm swell, that resplendent sky and then next to me that woman – all the joys of the earth, all its pleasures, everything most sweet, most intoxicating?

It was all the enchantment of a dream together with all the intense pleasures of reality. – I let myself be swept away by all those emotions, I advanced deeper into them with an insatiable joy, I grew more and more drunk on the voluptuous calm, that woman's gaze, that voice; I sank deep into my heart and discovered infinite pleasures in it.

How happy I was! – the happiness of the dusk darkening into nightfall, a happiness passing like the wave expiring, like the shore…

We returned. – We got out. I accompanied Maria back to her place; – I said not a word to her, I was timid; I was following her – dreaming of her, of the sound of her walking; and when she had gone in, I looked for a long time at the wall of her house lit up by the rays of the moon; I saw her light shining through the window-panes, and I turned round to look at it from time to time, as I made my way back along the strand; then when that light had disappeared, I said to myself, She's asleep.

And then all at once a thought came to assail me, a thought of rage and jealousy, Oh! no, she is not asleep. And in my soul I suffered all the torments of the damned. –

I thought of her husband, that vulgar, jovial man. – And the most hideous images presented themselves to my mind's eye; I was like those people who were left to die of starvation in cages, while surrounded by the most exquisite dishes. –

I was alone on the strand. Alone. She was no longer thinking of me. As I looked at that immense solitude before me, and that other solitude that was yet more terrible, I started to cry like a child – for near me, a few steps away, she was there, behind those walls that I was feasting my eyes on; she was there, beautiful and naked, with all the pleasures of night, all the graces of love, all the chastity of the marriage bed; that man had only to open his arms and she would come to him without him having to make an effort or wait; she would come to him; and they loved each other, they embraced; his were all the joys, all the delights were for him! My love under *his* feet, that whole woman, her head her throat her breasts, her body her soul – her smiles, her two arms enfolding him, her words of love: for him everything, for me nothing.

I started to laugh, for jealousy inspired me with obscene, grotesque thoughts, and then I sullied the two of them, I heaped on them the most bitter ridicule, and those images which had made me weep with envy – I tried to laugh with pity at them.

The tide was starting to go out again, and from place to place you could see big holes filled with water shining silvery in the moonlight, patches of still-wet sand covered with seaweed, here and there a few rocks sticking just above the surface of the water, or rising higher black or white; nets laid out and torn by the sea, which was withdrawing with a roar.

It was hot, I felt stifled; I went back to the room in my inn. – I tried to sleep: I could still hear the waves against the sides of the boat, I could hear the oar falling, I could hear Maria's voice talking; I had fire in my veins, the whole scene played itself out again and again before me – both the evening trip, and the walk back along the shore at night – I saw Maria in bed – and I stopped there. For the rest made me quiver. I had lava in my soul, I felt worn out by it all, and lying on my back I watched my candle burn down and its disc tremble on the ceiling; it was with a dazed stupor that I saw the tallow running down the copper candlestick and the black spark grow longer in the flame.

Finally daylight appeared – I went to sleep.

14

The time came to go. We separated without being able to bid her farewell. – She left the resort the same day as we did – it was a Sunday – she left in the morning, we left in the evening.

She left and I never saw her again. Farewell forever! She left like the dust of the road that flew up behind her. – How I have thought of it since – how many hours spent dumbfounded at the memory of her gaze, or the intonation of her words! – In the carriage I let my heart travel back down the road we had travelled, I imagined myself once more in the past that would never return; I thought of the sea, its waves, its shore, of all that I had just seen, of all that I had felt – the words spoken, the gestures, the actions, the slightest thing, it all throbbed with life; it was a chaos in my heart, an immense buzzing – a madness.

It had all passed like a dream. – Farewell forever to those lovely flowers of youth so quickly faded and towards which later on your thoughts return from time to time with simultaneous bitterness and pleasure! Eventually I saw the houses of my town, I returned home, everything there appeared to me deserted and doleful, empty and hollow. I started to live, to drink, to eat, to sleep.

Winter came, and I returned to school.

15

If I told you that I have loved other women I would be a despicable liar.

I thought I did, however; I forced myself to bind my heart to other passions, but it slid over them as if over ice.

When you are a child, you have read so many books about love, you find the very word so melodious, you dream of it so much, you have such a strong yearning to experience that feeling which makes you quiver when you read novels and dramas, that at every woman you see you say to yourself: isn't this love? You endeavour to love so as to make a man of yourself.

I have been no more immune than any other man from that childish weakness; I have sighed like an elegiac poet, and after many efforts I was quite astonished to find myself sometimes managing for a fortnight without having gone over to the woman I had chosen as the object of my dreams. All this child's vanity was erased when Maria appeared.

But I have to go back further – I have sworn an oath to say everything. The fragment you are about to read had been partly composed last December, before I had had the idea of writing the *Memoirs of a Madman*.

As it was to be an isolated piece I had placed it in the framework which follows...

Here it is, just as it was.

*

Among all the dreams of the past, the memories of days gone by and my reminiscences of youth, I have preserved a very small number with which I entertain myself in my hours of boredom. At the recollection of a name, all the characters return with their costumes and their language to play their roles as they played them in my life and I can see them performing their actions in front of me like a God entertaining himself by gazing at the worlds he has created. One especially – the first love, which was never violent nor passionate, later erased by other desires but still remaining in the depths of my heart like an ancient Roman way traversed by a wretched railway carriage.

It is the story of those first heartthrobs, those first sensations of indefinite and vague pleasures, of all the hazy things that happen in the soul of a child when he sees a woman's breasts, her eyes, and hears her songs and her words, it is that hotchpotch of emotion and reverie that I had to lay out like a corpse before a circle of friends who came one day in winter, in December, to get warm and laze around, to have a peaceful chat by the fireside while smoking their pipes whose acrid fumes were diluted by a glass of something or other.

After they had all arrived, and everyone had sat down, filled their pipes and their glasses, after we had gathered in a circle around the fire, one holding the tongs, the other using the bellows, a third stirring the ashes with his walking-stick, and everyone was fully occupied – I began.

'My dear friends,' I told them, 'you will be able to forgive a little something, an odd word of vanity that will slip into my story.'

Nods of agreement from all those present gave me permission to begin.

'I remember that it was a Thursday towards the month of November, two years ago (I was, I think, in the second form). – The first time I saw her, she was having lunch with my mother when I came rushing in, like a schoolboy who has been scenting Thursday's meal all week; she looked round; I barely greeted her for I was at the time so silly and childish that I couldn't see a woman – at least not any of those who didn't call me a child like the ladies, or a friend like the little girls – without blushing or rather without doing anything or saying anything.

'But thank God I have gained since in vanity and in impudence all that I have lost in innocence and candour.

'They were two young girls – sisters, friends of my sister, poor English girls who had been sent out of their boarding-house to get some fresh air, in the countryside, to be taken for drives, made to run around in the garden, and finally kept amused under the eyes of a nurse to calm and restrain the frolics of childhood.

'The oldest was fifteen, the second barely twelve – the latter was short and slender, her eyes were livelier, bigger and more beautiful than those of her older sister, but the older one had such a round and graceful head, her skin was so fresh, so rosy, her short teeth so white beneath her rosy lips, and the whole was so nicely framed by coils of pretty brown hair that you couldn't help giving her the prefer-ence. She was short and perhaps a little plump, this was her most visible defect; but what I found most enchanting about her was a childish, unpretentious grace, a fragrance of youth which filled the air around her with perfume – she had so much naivety and candour that even the most irreverent of people could not help admiring her.

'I still imagine I can see her, through the windows of my bedroom, running in the garden with some other friends. I can still see their silk dresses breaking into sudden ripples as they rustled round their heels, and their feet trotting along as they ran down the sanded garden paths, then com-ing to a stop out of breath, putting their arms round each other's waists and walking gravely along as they chatted, no doubt, about parties, dances, pleasures and love affairs, the poor girls!

'I soon got to know all of them well; at the end of four months I was kissing her like my sister, we were all on the friendliest terms. – I enjoyed talking with her so much! her foreign accent had something fine and delicate about it that made her voice as fresh as her cheeks.

'In addition there is in English manners a natural casualness and a neglect for all our accepted standards of behaviour that you could easily take for refined coquetry, but which is merely an attractive charm, like those will-o'-the-wisps which ceaselessly flee before you.

'Often we would go for walks together as a family, and I remember that one day in winter we went to see an old lady who lives on a hill overlooking the town; to reach her house you had to cross orchards planted with apple trees where the grass was tall and damp; the town was shrouded in mist and, from the top of our hill, we could see the serried roofs piled up and all covered with snow – and then the silence of the countryside, and in the distance the far-off sound of the tread of a cow or a horse whose hooves sank into the ruts.

'Passing through a gate painted white, her coat got caught in the thorns of the hedge, I went to free it; she said to me, "*Thank you*", with so much grace and ease of manner that I dreamt of it all day long.

'Then they started to run and their coats which the wind blew out behind them floated and rippled like a wave curling over – they stopped, out of breath. I can still remember their breathing panting in my ears as it came from between their white teeth in a hazy smoke.

'Poor girl! She was so kind and kissed me with such naivety. – '

*

'The Easter holidays arrived. We went to spend them in the country.

'I remember one day – the weather was warm, her belt

was hanging down, her dress was loose-waisted.

'We walked along together, treading underfoot the dew on the grass and the April flowers. She was carrying a book... it was poetry, I think; she dropped it. Our stroll continued.

'She had been running – I kissed her on the neck, my lips remained glued to that satiny skin, wet with a fragrant perspiration.

'I don't know what we talked about; the first things that came into our heads. – '

'This is where you're going to do something silly,' said one of the listeners, interrupting me.

'True, my friend, the heart is stupid.

'In the afternoon, my heart was filled with a sweet vague joy. – I daydreamed rapturously as I thought of her hair in curl-papers framing her vivacious eyes, and her already-developed bosom which I would always kiss as low as a scarf pulled high up *to preserve the decencies* would allow me. I made my way up into the fields; I went into the woods, I sat down in a ditch and I thought of her.

'I was lying on my stomach, pulling out stalks of grass and the April daisies, and when I looked up, the matt white sky formed above me a dome of blue that deepened down to the horizon behind the verdant meadows. As luck would have it, I had a paper and a pencil with me, and I wrote some poetry.'

Everyone started to laugh.

'The only poetry I have ever written in my life. There were perhaps thirty lines; it took me barely half an hour, as I always had an admirable ability to improvise when it came to silly little things of every kind. But this poetry was for the most part as false as a protestation of love. – And as shaky as virtue.

'I remember there was:

> *…when at evening*
> *She grows weary of playing games and sitting on the*
> *swing*

'I struggled in vain to depict an emotional warmth that I had only ever seen in books, then for no particular reason I moved on to a sombre, dignified melancholy worthy of the romantic hero Antony[5], although in reality my soul was imbued with innocence, and with a tender feeling composed of a mixture of silly nonsense, alluring memories and fragrances from the heart, and I said for no particular reason:

> *…My sorrow is bitter, my sadness is profound*
> *And I am buried in it, like a man laid in the ground.*

'The poetry wasn't even poetry, but I had the sense to burn it, a quirk that should nag the conscience of the majority of poets.

'I returned home and I found her playing on the round lawn. The room where the girls slept was next to mine, I could hear them laughing and chatting for a long time… whereas I… I soon went to sleep like her… in spite of all my efforts to stay awake as long as possible. For you have doubtless done as I did at the age of fifteen, you have once thought you were in love with that burning and frenzied love of the kind you've seen in books, whereas all you were suffering from was just a slight scratch on the epidermis of your heart left by that iron claw called passion, and you were blowing with all the strength of your imagination on that modest fire that was barely even alight.

'There is so much love of life in man! At the age of four, it's a love of horses, the sun, the flowers, shining weapons, soldier's uniforms. At ten, it's a love for the little girl who plays with you, at thirteen, love for a grown-up woman with a full bosom, for I recall that what teenage boys are crazy about is a woman's breasts, white and matt and as Marot says:

Titty like an egg all white
Satin titty fresh and bright.[6]

'I almost felt sick the first time I saw a woman's bare breasts. Finally at fourteen or fifteen, love for a young girl who comes round to your place. A bit more than a sister, less than a lover. Then at sixteen, love of another woman until you're twenty-five. Then perhaps you fall in love with the woman you will marry.

'Five years later you love the dancer who makes her gauze dress swirl around her fleshy thighs. Finally, at thirty-six, the love of being elected to parliament, of financial speculation, of honours; at fifty, love of dinner at the home of the mayor or the minister; at sixty, a love of the strumpet with her come-hither summons from behind the window-panes, whom you glance at impotently – a moment of nostalgia for the past.

'This is all true, isn't it? For my part, I have experienced all these kinds of love. – Not all of them, however, for I haven't yet lived all the years of my life, and every year in the life of many men is marked by a new passion – that for women, for gambling, for horses, for smart boots, for a new walking-stick, a new pair of glasses, carriages, positions of eminence.

'How many follies in a single man! – Oh, there's no question about it, a harlequin's outfit isn't more varied in its hues than is the human mind in its follies, and both of them come to the same end – that of both getting thread-bare and arousing laughter: the public pays money for its entertainment, the philosopher pays with his wisdom.'

'Get back to the story!' demanded one of the listeners, who, impassive up until then, took his pipe out of his mouth only so that he could direct at my digression, as it went up in smoke, the saliva of his reproach.

'I hardly know what to say after that, for there is a lacuna in the story, a line of verse missing from the elegy. Some time went by in this way. In May the mother of those girls came to France accompanying their brother. He was a charming boy, as blond as she was and sparkling with childish pranks and British pride.

'Their mother was a pale woman, lean and carefree. She was dressed in black, her manners and her words and her behaviour all had a carefree feel, a little indolent it's true, but resembling the Italian *far niente*. It was all however given more relish by the sheen of good taste you associate with an aristocratic polish. – She stayed in France for a month.

'I'

*

49

... then she went back home and we lived just as if we were all members of the same family, always together whenever we went out for a walk or on holiday, or took time off.

We were all brothers and sisters.

There were in our day-to-day relations so much grace and effusiveness, so much easy-going intimacy, that perhaps it degenerated into love – on her part at least and I had clear and repeated proof of the fact.

Often she would come up to me, put her arms round my waist – she would gaze at me, talk to me – the charming young thing! – she would ask me for books and plays, only a very few of which she ever returned; she would come up into my bedroom. I was quite embarrassed. Could I suppose a woman to have such boldness, or such naivety? One day she lay on my sofa in a perfectly equivocal position; I was sitting next to her, saying nothing.

To be sure, it was a critical moment; I didn't take advantage of it. –

I let her go.

At other times she would kiss me in tears. I couldn't believe that she really loved me. Ernest[7] was convinced of it, made me aware of it, called me a complete fool.

Whereas I was really at one and the same time shy – and uninvolved.

It was something sweet and childish, untarnished by any idea of possession but by that very fact deprived of energy. It was however too silly to be really platonic.

After a year their mother came to live in France – then at the end of a month she went back to England.

Her daughters had been taken out of boarding-school and were lodging with their mother in a deserted street, on the second floor.

During her journey, I would often see them at the windows. One day as I was going by, Caroline called to me, I went up.

She was alone. She threw herself into my arms and kissed me effusively. This was the last time, as since then she has got married.

Her drawing-master had been paying her frequent visits. They planned a wedding, it was all tied up and then abandoned a hundred times. – Her mother came back from England. Without her husband who no one ever heard mentioned.

Caroline got married in January. One day I met her with her husband – she barely acknowledged me.

Her mother has changed her lodgings and her way of life. – Now she receives at home tailors' assistants and students – she goes to masked balls and takes her young daughter there.

It's been eighteen months since we saw them.

So ended that liaison, which perhaps promised a passion with time but which ended all by itself.

*

Do I need to say that all this was to love what dusk is to broad daylight – and that Maria's eyes made the memory of that pale girl fade into nothing?

It was a low fire, and it has left only cold ashes.

16

This page is short, I wish it were even shorter; here is what happened.

Vanity pushed me into love; no: into pleasure; not even into that – into carnality.

I was mocked for my chastity – I would blush at the fact – I was ashamed of it, it weighed on me as if it had been a kind of corruption.

A woman presented herself to me. I took her – and I left her arms full of disgust and bitterness – but thereafter I could act like the Lovelace[8] of seedy cafés, spout as many obscenities as anyone else round a bowl of punch; I was a man now, I had gone off to indulge in a vice as if it were a duty – and then I had boasted about it. I was fifteen – I could talk about women and mistresses.

That woman – I conceived a real hatred for her; she would come to me – I would leave her; she would put on smiles which disgusted me as if they were a hideous grimace.

I felt remorse – as if Maria's love had been a religion I had profaned.

17

I wondered whether these were indeed the delights I had dreamt of, those fiery transports I had imagined in the virginity of my tender and childish heart. – Is that all it is? surely after that frigid enjoyment there should come another, more sublime, more immense, something divine – which makes you writhe in ecstasy? Oh! no, it was all over, I had gone and extinguished in the mire the sacred flame in my heart. – O Maria, I had gone and dragged through the mud the love your gaze had created, I had squandered it wilfully, on the first woman to come along, without love, without desire, impelled by a childish vanity – out of a calculating pride, so as not to blush at licentious talk, so as not to lose face at an orgy! Poor Maria.

I was weary, a profound loathing overcame my soul. – And I considered those momentary joys and those convulsions of the flesh pitiful.

I must have been perfectly wretched – I who was so proud of that love so elevated, of that sublime passion, I who regarded my heart as bigger and finer than those of other men, I – going off like them... Oh! no, not one of them perhaps did it for the same reasons: almost all of them were driven to it by their senses, they obeyed the instinct of nature in the same way a dog does; but there was much greater degradation involved in turning it into something calculated, in getting aroused by corruption, going off to throw yourself into the arms of a woman, handling her flesh, wallowing in the gutter so as to get up again and show off your stains.

And then I felt ashamed as at a cowardly profanation, I would like to have hidden from my own eyes the ignominy I had boasted of. –

I took myself back to the time when there was nothing dirty about the flesh for me, and when the prospect of desire showed me vague shapes and pleasures that my heart created.

No, no one will ever be able to describe all the mysteries of the virgin heart, all the things it feels, all the worlds to which it gives birth – how delightful its dreams are – how hazy and tender its thoughts – how bitter and cruel its disappointment.

To have loved, to have dreamt of heaven – to have seen everything that is most pure and sublime in the soul, and then to shackle oneself to all the heaviness of the flesh, all the languor of the body! – To have dreamt of heaven and to fall back down into the mud!

Who now will give me back all the things I have lost? my virginity, my dreams, my illusions, they are all things that have withered, poor flowers that the frost killed before they could blossom.

18

If I have felt moments of enthusiasm, it was to art that I owe them. – And yet, what a vanity is art! to want to depict man in a block of stone, or the soul in words, feelings by sounds, and nature on a varnished canvas!

A certain indefinable magical power is possessed by music. I have dreamt for weeks on end of the rhythmic beat of a melody or the broad outlines of a majestic chorus – there are sounds that pierce me to the quick and voices that have me melting in rapture.

I loved the orchestra with the rumble of its floods of harmony, its resounding vibrations and that immense vigour that seems endowed with muscles and dies at the end of the instrument's bow. My soul would follow the melody stretching out its wings to the infinite and rising up in a pure slow spiral like a fragrance towards heaven.

I loved the noise, the diamonds glittering in the lights, all those gloved women's hands holding flowers and applauding; I would watch the ballet dancers skipping about, their pink dresses floating, I heard their rhythmic footfalls – I watched their dimpling knees outlined as they bent forward.

At other times, meditating in front of works of genius, held by the chains with which they bind you, and then hearing the murmur of those voices with their flattering yelp, and that enchanting buzz of approval, I aspired to the destiny of those strong men who handle the crowd like lead, who can make it weep, groan, stamp its feet with enthusiasm. How immense must be their hearts for them to find room for the whole world there, and how abortive everything is in my nature! Convinced of my impotence and my sterility, I was overwhelmed by a jealous hatred, I told myself that it was nothing, that mere chance had dictated those words. – I hurled mud at the highest things I envied.

I had mocked God, I could easily laugh at mankind.

And yet this dark mood was only temporary, and I felt a real pleasure in contemplating genius shining in the home of art like a flower opening wide its rose-window of fragrance to a summer sun.

Art – art... what a beautiful thing is that vanity!

If there is on earth, and among all these things of nothing, a belief worthy of adoration, if there is anything holy, pure and sublime, anything answering that immoderate desire for the infinite and the vague that we call the soul, it is art.

And what littleness! a stone – a word – a sound – the arrangement of all those things, that we call the sublime.

I would like something that no longer needed expression or shape. – Something as pure as a fragrance, as strong as stone, as elusive as a song; if only it could be all of that and yet none of those individual things.

Everything seems to me limited, shrunk, abortive in nature.

Man with his genius and his art is nothing but a miserable ape of something higher.

I would like to find beauty in the infinite and all I find there is doubt.

19

Oh! the infinite, the infinite, that immense abyss, a spiral rising from the deepest depths right up to the highest regions of the unknown – an old idea in which we are all turning round and round, seized by vertigo – the abyss each person has at heart, an incommensurable abyss, a bottomless abyss.

In vain, for many days and nights on end, we will ask ourselves in our anguish: what is this word... God, eternity, the infinite? – and there we go round in circles, swept away by a wind of death, like the leaf blown along by the hurricane – it is as if the infinite then takes pleasure in lulling us ourselves in that immensity of doubt. And yet we always tell ourselves: after many centuries, after thousands of years, when everything has been worn out, there must be a limit there.

Alas, eternity rises before us and we are afraid of it – afraid of that thing which must last for such a long time, we who last for so little.

For such a long time!

Doubtless when the world no longer exists (how I would like to be alive then – living without nature or men – what grandeur in that void!), doubtless there will be darkness then – a little burnt ash which will have been the earth and perhaps a few drops of water – the sea.

Heavens! nothing more – emptiness – only the void spread out across the vast expanse like a shroud!

Eternity, eternity! – will it last forever?... forever, without end?

And yet what remains, the smallest scrap of the world's debris, the last breath of a dying creation, the void itself, will necessarily be weary of existing. – Everything will call for total destruction.

This idea of something without end makes us grow pale. – Alas! and we will be in it, all of us now living – and this immensity will sweep us along.

What will we be? A nothing – not even a breath of air.

I have long thought of the dead in their coffins, the protracted centuries they spend like that under the earth filled with rumours and cries, and they so calm, in their rotten wooden boxes, their gloomy silence interrupted, at times, either by a hair falling, or by a worm slithering by, over a shred of flesh. How they sleep there, lying silent – under the earth – under the flowering turf!

And yet, at wintertime, they must be cold under the snow.

Oh! if only they could awaken then – if they could come back to life and see all the tears with which their funeral sheets were bedewed now dried, all those sobs stifled – all those grimaces at an end. – They would be filled with horror at this life that they bewailed as they left it – and they would quickly return to the nothingness so calm and so true.

To be sure it is possible to live, and even die, without

having once asked oneself what life and death are.

But for the man who watches the leaves trembling in the wind's breath, the rivers meandering through the meadows, life twisting and turning and swirling through things, men living, doing good and evil, the sea rolling its waves and the sky with its expanse of lights, and who asks himself why these leaves are there, why the water flows, why life itself is such a terrible torrent plunging towards the boundless ocean of death in which it will lose itself, why men walk about, labour like ants, why the tempest, why the sky so pure and the earth so foul – these questions lead to a darkness from which there is no way out.

And doubt comes afterwards; it is... something that cannot be said but can be felt. Man then is like that traveller lost amid the sands searching everywhere for a route to lead him to the oasis but seeing only the desert.

Doubt is life – action, words, nature, death. Doubt is in it all.

Doubt is death for souls; it is a leprosy that seizes on worn-out races; it is an illness that comes from knowledge and leads to madness.

Madness is the doubt of reason.

Perhaps it *is* reason.

Who can prove it one way or the other?

20

There are poets whose souls are filled with fragrance and flowers, who regard life as the daybreak of heaven, and others who are filled with nothing but darkness, bitterness and anger – there are painters who see everything in blue, others who see it all in yellow or all in black. Each of us has a prism through which we observe the world, happy is the one who can find cheerful colours and merry things in it. –

There are men who see in the world nothing other than a title to be gained, or women, or the bank, a fine name, a destiny: follies. –

I know some who can see only railways, markets, or live-stock. Some discern in it a sublime plan, others an obscene farce.

And the former would ask you what after all is the *obscene*? A difficult question to answer, like all questions.

I would just as much like to give the geometrical definition of a fine pair of boots or a beautiful woman, two things of great importance.

The people who see our globe as a big or small heap of mud are singular characters and difficult to pin down.

You come to talk with one of those despicable people, people who don't call themselves philanthropists and won't vote for the demolition of cathedrals, and are unafraid of being labelled reactionary Carlists[9]. But soon you stop short or confess that you have been beaten, for the former are unprincipled people, who consider virtue to be a mere word, and the world a piece of buffoonery. Hence they set out to consider everything from a sordid point of view, they smile in disdain at the most beautiful things and when you talk to them about philanthropy, they shrug and tell you that philanthropy is shown by contributing to a fund for the poor.

What a fine thing is a list of names in a newspaper!

What a strange thing is this diversity of opinions, of sys-tems, of beliefs and of follies.

When you talk to certain people, they suddenly stop in

dismay and ask you: What, you are going to deny that? You're capable of doubting that? can one revoke the plan of the universe and the duties of mankind? And if unfortunately your gaze has betrayed your soul's dreams – they suddenly stop short and leave their logical victory there, like those children who, frightened by an imaginary ghost, shut their eyes and dare not peep.

Open your eyes – man, weak and yet full of pride, poor ant crawling with such effort across your speck of dust, you call yourself free and great, you respect yourself, despite being so vile all life long, and derisively no doubt you hail your rotten and transient body – and then you think that such a fine life, hectically driven in this way between the scrap of pride that you call greatness and that sordid self-interest that is the essence of your society, will be crowned by immortality. Immortality for you, more lecherous than a monkey, and more savage than a tiger, and more creeping than a serpent – come on now! make me a paradise for the monkey the tiger and the serpent, for lust cruelty baseness – a paradise for egotism, eternity for this dust, immortality for this nothingness!

You boast of being free, of being able to do what you call good and evil, doubtless so as to be condemned all the more quickly, for what good could you ever do? is there a single one of your gestures which is not stimulated by pride or calculated out of self-interest?

You, free! – From your birth onwards you are subject to all the infirmities of your father, you receive with life the seed of all your vices, of your very stupidity, of all that will make you judge the world, yourself, and all that surrounds you, in accordance with that term of comparison, that measure you carry within yourself. You are born with a narrow spirit, with ready-made ideas, or ideas that will be ready made for you, about good and evil. You will be told that one must love one's father and look after him in his old age, you will do both and yet you didn't need anyone to teach you to do it, did you? It is an innate virtue like the need to eat. While on the other side of the mountain where you were born your brother will be taught to kill his father when he is old, and he will kill him, for that, he thinks, is natural, and it was not necessary for anyone to teach him to do it. You will be brought up by people who tell you that you must be very careful not to love carnally your sister or your mother, while you are descended like everyone from an incest, for the first man and the first woman, they and their children, were brothers and sisters; while the sun sets on other peoples who regard incest as a virtue and parricide as a duty. Are you already free in the principles by which you will govern your behaviour, is it you who presides over your upbringing, is it you who chose to be born with a character happy or sad, consumptive or robust, gentle or savage, moral or depraved?

But first of all why were you born? did you choose to be? were you consulted on the matter? So you were born inevitably because your father, one day, returned from an orgy heated by wine and licentious chatter and your mother took advantage of this, setting in motion all those tricks of a woman impelled by the fleshly, bestial instincts given to her by nature when it gave her a soul, and she managed to arouse the man that prostitutes had been draining dry ever since his teens. Whatever you may be, you were to begin with something as dirty as saliva and more fetid than urine, then you underwent metamorphoses like a worm, and finally you came into the world, almost lifeless, crying, howling and shutting your eyes as if from hatred of that sun you called for so many times.

You are given something to eat. – You grow and develop like the leaf – it is mere chance if the wind does not sweep you away early, for to how many things are you subject? To air, to fire, to light, to day, to night, to cold, to heat, to everything that surrounds you, everything that exists: all of this masters you, holds you in thrall. You love verdure and flowers, and you are sad when they wither, you love your dog, you weep when it dies, a spider comes towards you, you draw back in horror, you shudder sometimes at the sight of your shadow and when your thought itself dives into the mysteries of nothingness, you are dismayed and you are afraid of doubt.

You say you are free and every day you act at the behest of a thousand things, you see a woman and you love her, you die of love for her: are you free to quieten that pulsing blood, to calm that burning head, to repress your heart, to pacify the ardour that devours you? Are you free of your thought? A thousand chains hold you back, a thousand stimuli drive you on, a thousand obstacles bring you to a halt. You see a man for the first time, one of his features shocks you, and all your life long you feel aversion for this man for whom you would perhaps have felt the greatest affection if he had not had such a big nose. – You have a poor digestion and treat with brutality the person you would otherwise have greeted with benevolence. And from all these facts flow or are linked just as unavoidably other series of facts, whence others derive in turn.

Are you the creator of your physical and moral constitution? No. You could be in full control of it only if you had fashioned and modelled it as you pleased.

You call yourself free because you have a soul – firstly it is you who made this discovery that you cannot even define; an intimate voice says yes – firstly you are lying: a voice tells you that you are weak and you feel within yourself an immense void that you would like to fill with all the things you throw into it. Even if you thought you did have a soul, are you sure? Who told you? When having been torn apart by two opposing feelings, after a long period of hesitation and doubt, you incline towards one of the feelings, you believe you were the master of your choice. But to be master it would be necessary to have no inclination at all. Are you master enough to do good if a taste for evil has implanted itself in your heart, if you have been born with bad inclinations that have been fostered by your upbringing? And if you are virtuous, if you hold crime in horror, will you be able to do it? are you free to do good or evil? since it is the feeling for good that always controls you, you cannot do evil.

This battle is the struggle between two inclinations, and if you do evil it is because you are more depraved than virtuous and the stronger fever has gained the upper hand.

When two men fight, it is certain that the weaker, the less adroit, and the less supple will be vanquished by the stronger, the more adroit, and the more supple – however long the struggle lasts there will always be one who is vanquished. The same goes for your inner nature: even when what you feel to be good wins, is this always a victory for justice? is what you judge good the absolute, immutable, eternal good?

All is thus darkness around man, all is empty and he would like something fixed – he himself spins through this vague immensity where he would like to find a firm footing – he clings to everything and everything fails him: fatherland, freedom, belief, God, virtue, he has seized it all and it has fallen from his hands – like a madman who drops a crystal vase and laughs at all the fragments he has made.

But man has an immortal soul made in God's image – two ideas for which he has shed his blood, two ideas which he cannot understand: a soul – a God, but ideas of which he is convinced.

This soul is an essence around which our physical being rotates as does the earth around the sun. – This soul is noble, for being a spiritual principle, and not earthly, there cannot be anything low or base about it. And yet isn't it thought that directs our bodies, isn't it that which makes us lift our arms when we want to kill? isn't it thought that animates our flesh? could it be that spirit is the principle of evil and the body its agent?

Let us see how elastic and flexible this soul is, how soft and pliable, how easily it crumples beneath the body that weighs down on it or leans on the body which obediently bows, how venal and base this soul is, how it creeps, how it flatters, how it lies, how it deceives. – It is the soul that sells the body, the hand, the head and the tongue – it is the soul that craves blood and demands gold, forever insatiable and coveting everything in its infinite longings – it is in the midst of us, like a thirst, a kind of ardour, a fire devouring us, a pivot which forces us to rotate around it.

You are great! man! not by the body, doubtless, but by

this spirit that has made you, so you say, the king of nature; you are great, masterful and strong.

Every day indeed you upturn the earth, you dig canals, you build palaces, you encase rivers in stone, you pick grass, you knead it and eat it, you stir the ocean with the keel of your vessels and you find all of that beautiful, you think yourself better than the wild beasts that you eat, freer than the leaf swept away by the winds, greater than the eagle who hovers over your towers, stronger than the earth from which you draw your bread and your diamonds and the ocean across which you sail, but alas! – the earth that you upturn returns to its place, your canals are destroyed, the rivers invade your fields and your cities, the stones of your palaces come apart and collapse under their own weight, ants scurry across your crowns and your thrones, all your fleets are unable to leave any more traces of their passage on the surface of the ocean than a drop of rain or a bird's wing-beat, and you yourself pass across that age-old ocean without leaving any more trace of yourself than your ship leaves on the waves. You think yourself great because you work without respite, but this work is a proof of your weakness – you were thus condemned to learn all these useless things in the sweat of your brow; you were a slave before birth, and wretched before you had begun to live. You look at the stars with a smile of pride because you have given them names, because you have calculated their distance as if you wanted to measure the infinite and enclose space within the bounds of your spirit. But you are wrong! Who tells you that behind these worlds of light, there are not yet others infinite in number, and so on forever? Your calculations come to an end perhaps at a height of a few feet, just where a new scale of things begins. Do you your-self understand the value of the words you use... expanse, space? They are vaster than you and your entire globe.

You are great and you die, like the dog and the ant, with more regret than they do, and then you rot, and I ask you, when the worms have eaten you, when your body has dis-solved in the dankness of the tomb, and your dust is no more, where are you, man? Where even is your soul – that soul which was the driving force behind your actions, which delivered your heart up to hatred, to envy, to all the passions, this soul which sold you and made you commit so many base actions, where is it? Is there a place holy enough to receive it?

You respect yourself and honour yourself as a God – you have invented the idea of the dignity of man, an idea that nothing in nature could conceive at the sight of you, you desire to be honoured, and you honour yourself, you even want this body so vile during its life to be honoured when it no longer exists. You want people to take off their hats out of respect for your human carcass – which is rotten with corruption, although it is even purer than you were when you were alive. That is your greatness.

Greatness of dust, majesty of nothingness!

21

I went back two years later, you know where, she was no longer there.

Her husband had come alone with another woman, and he had left two days before my arrival.

I returned to the shore – how empty it was! From there I could see the grey wall of Maria's house – what isolation!

So I went back into the same room I have told you about, it was full but none of the faces was still there, the tables were taken by people that I had never seen, Maria's was occupied by an old woman who was propped up at that same place where so often her elbow had rested.

I stayed there in this way for a fortnight – there were a few days of bad weather and rain which I spent in my room where I could hear the rain falling on the slates, the distant sound of the sea and from time to time some sailors' cries on the quayside. I remembered all those old things that the sight of the same places brought back to life.

I saw the same ocean with the same waves, it was as immense as ever, roaring gloomily against its rocks, that same village with its piles of mud, its shells that you tread underfoot and its tiered houses – but all that I had loved, all that surrounded Maria, the beautiful sun shining through the shutters and making her skin glow gold, the air enfolding her, the people going past her, all of that had gone for good. Oh! how I would simply like just one of those days – days without equal – so I could go in without changing a thing!

Ah, will none of it ever return? I feel how empty my heart is, for all these men around me create a desert in which I am dying.

I remembered those long warm summer afternoons when I would talk to her without her suspecting that I loved her and when her indifferent glance pierced me like a ray of love penetrating right into my heart. And how could she have seen that I loved her, for at that time I did not love her, and all that I have just told you was a lie: it was now that I loved her, that I desired her, that alone on the shore, in the woods or in the fields, I summoned her into being, she walking right there next to me, talking to me, looking at me. When I lay down on the grass, and watched the grass bending in the wind and the wave beating on the sand, I thought of her, and I reconstructed in my heart all the scenes in which she had acted, spoken. These memories were a passion.

If I recalled having seen her walking in a place I would go walking there myself – I wanted to rediscover the timbre of her voice so as to delight my own ears, it was impossible. How many times did I walk past her house and look at her window!

So I spent that fortnight in a lovesick contemplativeness – dreaming of her. I remember heartbreaking things; one day I was coming back, towards dusk, I was walking across pasture-land covered with cattle; I walked quickly, I could hear nothing but the sound of my steps swishing through the grass, I was looking down at the ground; this regular movement sent me to sleep, as it were, I thought I could hear Maria walking at my side, she was holding my arm and turning her head to look at me – it was she who was walking through the grass; I was fully aware that it was a hallucination that I myself was bringing to life, but I could not stop myself smiling at it and I felt happy; – I looked up, the weather was overcast; before me, on the horizon, the sun was setting in splendour beneath the waves, an upsurge of fire could be seen branching out and disappearing under the thick black clouds billowing laboriously over them, and then a reflection of this setting sun reappeared further behind me in a clear blue part of the sky.

When I came in sight of the sea the sun had almost

disappeared, its disc was half submerged in the water and a delicate pink hue continued to spread out and fade away skywards.

On another occasion I was returning on horseback along the shore. I looked mechanically at the waves whose foam washed the hooves of my mare, I looked at the pebbles that she kicked up as she walked along and at her hooves sinking in the sand. The sun had just suddenly disappeared. – And there was a dark colour on the waves as if something black had been hovering over them. To my right were rocks between which the foam was whipped up by the wind like a sea of snow, the gulls were passing over my head and I could see their white wings dipping right down towards that dark, gloomy water – nothing will express how beautiful it was, that sea, that shore with its sand scattered with shells, with its rocks covered with damp seaweed, and the white foam curling over them in the breeze.

I could tell you many other things, of even greater beauty and sweetness, if I could relate all that I felt of love, of ecstasy, of nostalgia. – Can you express in words the beating of the heart, can you express a tear, and depict its damp crystal that bathes the eye in a languor of love, can you express all that you feel in a single day?

Poor human weakness! with your words, your languages, your sounds, you speak and stammer – you define God, the heaven and the earth, chemistry and philosophy, and you cannot express, with your language, all the joy that you derive from a naked woman – or a plum pudding.

22

O Maria, Maria, beloved angel of my youth, you whom I saw when my feelings were still fresh, you whom I loved with such a sweet love, so full of fragrance, of tender daydreams, farewell.

Farewell – other passions will return – I will forget you perhaps – but you will always remain in the depths of my heart, for the heart is a soil on which each passion turns over, stirs and churns up the ruins of the others. Farewell.

Farewell, and yet how deeply I would have loved you, how I would have embraced you – held you tight in my arms. Ah! my soul melts in raptures, at all the follies that my love invents. Farewell.

Farewell, and yet I will always think of you; – I will be hurled into the maelstrom of the world – I will die there perhaps crushed beneath the feet of the crowd, torn to pieces. Where am I going? what will become of me? I would like to be old, have white hair – no, I would like to be as handsome as the angels, to have fame and genius, and lay it all at your feet so that you can walk over it all, but I have none of it – and you looked at me as coldly as at a lackey or a beggar.

And as for me, do you know that I have not spent a night, or a day, or an hour, without thinking of you, without seeing you emerging from beneath the waves, with your black hair on your shoulders – your brown skin with its beads of salt water, your clothes streaming and your white foot with its pink toenails sinking into the sand – and this vision is always present and always murmuring within my heart? – Oh! no, everything is empty.

Farewell, and yet when I saw you if only I had been four

or five years older, a little bolder... perhaps... oh! no, I blushed every time you looked at me. Farewell.

23

When I hear the bells chiming and the knell tolling its dirge, I feel in my soul a vague sadness, something indefinable and dreamy like dying vibrations.

A series of thoughts opens up at the mournful ringing of the death-knell, it seems to me that I can see the world on its most splendid festival days with cries of triumph, chariots and crowns, and above it all an eternal silence and an eternal majesty. –

My soul soars up towards eternity and infinity and hovers in the ocean of doubt at the sound of this voice announcing death.

A voice as measured and cold as tombs, and which yet rings out at every festival, weeps at every bereavement – I love to let myself be deafened by your harmony, which muffles the hubbub of towns; I love, in the fields, on the hills made golden with ripe wheat, to hear the frail sounds of the village bell singing in the middle of the countryside, while the insect makes a shrill noise under the grass and the bird murmurs amidst the leaves.

I have often remained, in the winter, on those sunless days, when the light gleams wan and gloomy, listening to all the bells ringing for the services – from every side there emerged voices rising towards the sky in a tracery of harmony – and I let my thoughts follow the rhythm of that gigantic instrument – they were vast, infinite, I could feel within myself sounds, melodies, echoes of another world, immense things that were dying too.

O bells, you will ring also for my death, and a minute later for a baptism! So you too are as derisive as all the rest, and a lie like life – all of whose phases you announce: baptism, marriage, death – poor lonely bronze bell, perched amidst the winds, and which would be so useful as lava flow on a battlefield, or melted down to make shoes for horses.

Bibliomania

A short while ago, there lived in a street in Barcelona[1], narrow and sunless, one of those men of pale brow and lacklustre, sunken eye, one of those strange and satanic beings, of the kind that Hoffmann used to dig up in his daydreams.

It was Giacomo the bookseller; he was thirty, and people already considered him old and worn out. He was tall, but he stooped like an old man; his hair was long, but white; his hands were strong and vigorous, but emaciated and covered with wrinkles; his outfit was wretched and tattered; he had a gauche and embarrassed appearance, his physiognomy was pale, sad, ugly, and even insignificant. He was rarely seen in the streets except on days when rare and curious books were being auctioned off. Then, he was no longer the same indolent and ridiculous man. His eyes lit up, he ran, he walked, he hopped up and down, he could hardly manage to contain his joy, his anxieties, his anguishes and his doubts; he would come back home panting, winded, out of breath. He would take the cherished book, look longingly at it, gaze at it lovingly, as a miser loves his treasure, a father his daughter, a king his crown.

This man had never spoken to anyone other than second-hand booksellers and junk-shop owners. He was taciturn and dreamy, sombre and gloomy; he had only one idea, one love, one passion: books. And this love and this passion inflamed him within, consumed his days, devoured his whole life.

Often, at night, his neighbours could see, through the bookseller's windows, a light that flickered, then came nearer, moved away, rose, and then sometimes went out. Then they would hear a knock at their door, and it was

Giacomo who had come to relight his candle which the mere turn of a page had extinguished.

Those feverish, ardent nights he would spend in his books; he ran round his stores, he moved along the galleries of his library in ecstasy and ravishment, then he would stop, his hair in disarray, his eyes fixed and sparkling. His hands would tremble as he touched the books on the shelves; they were hot and damp. He would take a book, turn over its leaves, feel its paper, examine its gilding, its cover, its lettering, its ink, its folds, and the arrangement of the designs for the word *finis*. Then he would change its place, putting it on a higher shelf, and he spent entire hours gazing at its title and shape.

Then he would go off to his manuscripts, for they were his beloved children; he would take one, the oldest, the most dog-eared, the dirtiest; he would look at its parchment with love and happiness; he would smell its holy and venerable dust; then his nostrils would flare with joy and pride, and a smile came to his lips.

Oh! he was happy, this man; happy in the middle of all this knowledge, the moral significance and literary value of which he barely comprehended; he was happy in the midst of all these books, letting his eyes rove over the gilded letters, over the dog-eared pages, over the stained parchment. He loved knowledge as a blind man loves daylight.

No! it was not knowledge that he loved, it was the form and expression it took. He loved a book, because it was a book; he loved its smell, its shape, its title. What he loved in a manuscript was its old illegible date, the Gothic letters, bizarre and strange, the heavy gilding that embellished the drawings; it was those pages covered with dust, a dust whose sweet and tender fragrance he breathed in with rapture. It was that lovely word *finis*, surrounded by two Cupids set upon a ribbon, or leaning against a fountain, or engraved on a tomb, or resting in a basket between the roses and golden apples and the blue bouquets.

This passion had absorbed him entirely: he hardly ate, he no longer slept; but he dreamt for entire days and nights of his *idée fixe*: books. He dreamt how completely divine, sublime, and beautiful a royal library must be, and he dreamt of assembling for himself one as big as a king's. How freely he breathed, how proud and powerful he was when his gaze travelled far down the immense galleries where it lost itself in books! did he lift up his head? books! did he bend down? books! to the right, to the left, more books!

In Barcelona he was taken for a strange and infernal man, a scholar or a sorcerer.

He could barely read. Nobody dared speak to him, so severe and pale was his brow; he had a savage, perfidious appearance, and yet he never touched a child with intent to harm him; it is true that he never gave alms.

He kept all his money, all his property, all his emotions for books; he had been a monk, and, for them, he had abandoned God. Later on he sacrificed for them that which men hold most dear, after their God: money; then he gave for them what is most dear to men, after money: his soul.

For some time past, in particular, he had been spending longer and longer awake at night. His night-light was seen burning over his books ever later, the reason being that he had a new treasure, a manuscript.

One morning, there came into his shop a young student

from Salamanca. He appeared rich, for two footmen were holding his mule at Giacomo's door. He was wearing a red velvet toque, and there were rings glittering on his fingers.

However, he did not have that self-satisfied, vacant air habitual with people who have valets in braid, fine clothes, and an empty head. No, this man was a scholar, but a rich scholar. In other words a man who, in Paris, writes on a mahogany table, has gilt-edged books, embroidered slippers, Chinese curios, a dressing-gown, a golden clock, a cat sleeping on his carpet, and two or three women who make him read his poetry, his prose, and his short stories, who tell him, 'You are a man of wit', and merely find him fatuous. This gentleman's manners were polite. As he entered he greeted the librarian, bowed deeply and said to him affably:

'Do you not have any manuscripts here, sir?'

The bookseller became embarrassed, and replied stammeringly:

'But, my lord, who told you?'

'Nobody, but I just suppose you do.'

And he set down on the bookseller's counter a bag full of gold, which he jingled with a smile, like any man touching money that belongs to him.

'My lord,' replied Giacomo, 'it is true that I do, but I don't sell them; I keep them.'

'And why is that? what do you do with them?'

'Why, my good lord?' – At this point he became red with anger. 'What do I do with them? Oh! no, you can't possibly know what a manuscript is!'

'Excuse me, Master Giacomo, I am an expert in the matter, and, just to prove it to you, I will tell you that you have here the *Chronicle of Turpin!*[2]

'Me? oh! someone has misinformed you, my lord.'

'No, Giacomo,' replied the gentleman, 'you can rest assured; I don't want to steal it from you, but buy it off you.'

'Never!'

'Oh! you will sell it to me,' replied the scholar, 'for you do have it here, it was sold at Ricciami's on the day he died.'

'Very well! yes, my lord, I do have it; it's my treasure, it's my life. Oh! you will never wrest it from me! Listen, I'm going to tell you a secret. Baptisto, you know, Baptisto, the bookseller who lives on the Royal Square, my rival and my enemy, well! *he* doesn't have it, and I do!'

'How much do you think it's worth?'

Giacomo hesitated for a long time, and replied proudly:

'Two hundred pistoles, my lord.'

He looked triumphantly at the young man, as if to tell him, 'You'll be off now, it's too expensive for you, and yet I'm not going to let you have it for any less.' He was wrong, for the young man, showing him the bag, said:

'Here are three hundred.'

Giacomo went pale; he was on the point of fainting.

'Three hundred pistoles?' he repeated, 'but I'm a madman, my lord; I wouldn't sell it for four hundred.'

The student started to laugh, and, digging into his pocket, from which he drew two other bags, said:

'Very well! Giacomo, here are five hundred. Oh! no, so you don't want to sell it then, Giacomo? But I'll have it, I'll have it today, this very instant, I must have it. Even if I have to sell this ring, given to me in a long loving kiss, even if I have to sell my diamond-encrusted sword, my town houses and my palaces, even if I have to sell my soul! I must have that book. Yes, I must have it, at all costs, at any price! In a week's time I am defending my thesis at Salamanca. I must have that book so as to be a doctor; I must be a doctor so as to become an archbishop; I must have scarlet on my shoulders so as to have the tiara on my brow!'

Giacomo went up to him and looked at him with admiration and respect as the only man who could ever have understood him.

'Listen, Giacomo,' interrupted the gentleman, 'I'm going to tell you a secret that will make your fortune and assure your happiness. Here there is a man, and that man lives in the Moorish quarter; there is a book; it is the *Mystery of Saint Michael*.'

'The *Mystery of Saint Michael*?' said Giacomo, uttering a cry of joy, 'oh! thank you! you have saved my life.'

'Quick! give me *The Chronicle of Turpin*.'

Giacomo ran over to a shelf; there, he suddenly stopped, forced himself to grow pale, and said with astonishment:

'But, my lord, I don't have it.'

'Oh! Giacomo, your tricks are really crude, and your eyes belie your words.'

'Oh! my lord, I swear to you; I don't have it.'

'Come now! you're an old madman, Giacomo; look, here are six hundred pistoles.'

Giacomo took the manuscript and gave it to this young man:

'Take care of it,' he said, as the latter made his way out laughing and telling his valets as he climbed onto his mule:

'You know that your master is a madman, but he has just

swindled a fool. The credulous idiot!' he repeated with a laugh, 'he thinks I'm going to be Pope!'

And poor Giacomo was left in sadness and despair, leaning his burning brow against the window-panes of his shop as he wept with rage, and watching in pain and grief as his manuscript, the object of his care and his affections, was carried off by the gentleman's coarse valets.

'Oh! curse you, you man from hell! curse you! curse you a hundred times, you have stolen from me all that I loved on earth, where I will no longer be able to live. I know he has deceived me, the vile man, he has deceived me! If that were the case, oh! I would take my vengeance. No! Quick, let's run over to the Moorish quarter. If that man were to ask me for a sum I don't have, what then? Oh! it's enough to be the death of me!'

He took the money the student had left on his counter and ran out.

As he made his way through the streets, he took in nothing of his surroundings; it all passed in front of his eyes like a phantasmagoria whose riddle he could not solve; he could hear neither the footfalls of the passers-by, nor the noise of the wheels on the cobbles; he was not thinking of anything, not dreaming of or seeing anything, except for one thing: books. He thought of the *Mystery of Saint Michael*, he pictured it in his imagination, broad and slender, its parchment adorned with gold letters; he tried to guess the number of pages that it must contain. His heart was beating violently like that of a man waiting for his death sentence. At last he arrived.

The student had not deceived him!!!

On an old Persian carpet full of holes were scattered on

the ground a dozen or so old books. Giacomo, without speaking to the man who was sleeping at one side, lying on the ground like the books, and snoring in the sunshine, fell on his knees, started to run an anxious and attentive eye over the spines of all the books; then he stood up pale and downcast; he awoke the bookseller with a cry, and asked him:

'Hey, friend, don't you have here the *Mystery of Saint Michael*?'

'What?' said the merchant opening his eyes, 'can't you talk about a book I do have? Look!'

'You idiot!' said Giacomo, stamping his foot, 'do you have any others apart from those?'

'Yes, look, here you are.'

And he showed him a little bundle of unbound books tied together with string. Giacomo snapped the string angrily and read their titles in a second.

'Hell!' he said, 'that's not it. You haven't sold it, by any chance? Oh! if you possess it, give it me, give it me! A hundred pistoles... two hundred... as much as you like.'

The bookseller looked at him in astonishment:

'Ah! perhaps you mean a little book I gave yesterday, for eight maravedis, to the priest of Oviedo cathedral?'

'Can you remember the title of that book?'

'No.'

'Wasn't it the *Mystery of Saint Michael*?'

'Yes, that's it.'

Giacomo staggered a few steps away, and fell into the dust, like a man exhausted by an apparition preying on him.

When he came round, it was evening, and the sun,

which was glowing red on the horizon, was sinking; he picked himself up and returned home feeling sick and desperate.

A week later, Giacomo had not forgotten his unhappy deception, his wound was still fresh and bleeding; he had not slept a wink for three nights, for this was the day on which was to be sold the first book that had been printed in Spain, the only copy in the kingdom.

He had wanted to possess it for a long time. So he was happy, the day they announced to him that its owner was dead. But an anxiety was gnawing at his soul: Baptisto could buy it; Baptisto, who, for some time, had been filching from him, not his regular customers (he cared little enough about that), but all the rarities and novelties that appeared; Baptisto whose renown he hated with an artist's hatred. This man was becoming a burden to him. It was always he who swiped the manuscripts at the public sales: he would bid higher and get his prize. Oh! how often had the poor monk, in his dreams of ambition and pride, how often had he seen coming towards him the long hand of Baptisto, passing through the crowd, as on auction days, to snatch away a treasure that he had dreamt of for so long, that he had lusted after with so much love and selfish desire!

How many times too he was tempted to bring off with a crime what neither money nor patience had been able to achieve; but he repressed this idea in his heart, trying to deaden the hatred he bore that man, and fell asleep over his books.

As soon as the next morning came, he was outside the house in which the auction was to take place; he was there before the auditor, before the public, and before the sun.

As soon as the doors opened, he rushed to the stairs, ran up into the hall, and asked for that book. They showed it to him: it was already a real joy.

Oh! never had he seen such a beautiful book, or one that he took such delight in; it was a Latin Bible, with Greek commentaries. He gazed at it and admired it more than all the others; he clutched it between his fingers with a bitter laugh, like a man dying of starvation at the sight of gold.

Never had he felt such strong desire, either: oh! how he would have liked then, even at the cost of all that he possessed, of his books, of his manuscripts, of his six hundred pistoles, at the cost of his blood, oh! how he would have liked to have that book, to sell everything, everything so as to have that book; to have it alone, but securely in his possession; to be able to show it to the whole of Spain, with an insulting and pitying laugh for the king, for the princes, for the scholars, for Baptisto, and to say: 'It's mine! this book is mine!' – and to hold it in his hands all his life long; to finger it as he was touching it, to smell it as he could smell it now, and to possess it as he was gazing on it!

Finally the time came. Baptisto was present, his face serene, looking calm and peaceful. They came to the book. At first Giacomo offered twenty pistoles. Baptisto said nothing and did not look at the Bible. Already the monk was reaching out to lay his hands on the book, which had cost him so little pain and anguish, when Baptisto began to say: 'Forty.' Giacomo saw with horror his antagonist becoming more and more heated as the price rose higher and higher.

'Fifty!' he cried with all his strength.

'Sixty!' replied Baptisto.

'A hundred!'

'Four hundred!'

'Five hundred!' added the monk enraged.

And while he was hopping up and down with impatience and anger, Baptisto was affecting an ironic and malicious calm. Already the shrill, broken voice of the auctioneer had repeated three times: 'five hundred', already Giacomo was feeling his happiness secured once more, when a breath from a man's lips made him faint away. For the bookseller of the Royal Square, thrusting his way through the crowd, started to say: 'Six hundred!' The auctioneer's voice repeated: 'six hundred', four times, and no further voice replied. But at one of the ends of the table could be seen a man, with a pale brow and trembling hands, a man laughing bitterly with the laughter of the damned in Dante. He lowered his head, and his hand was thrust into his bosom; when he took it out, it was hot and wet, for there was flesh and blood at the tip of the fingernails.

The book was passed from hand to hand towards Baptisto. This book passed in front of Giacomo, he smelt its odour, he saw it moving for a swift instant before his eyes, then stop at a man who took it and opened it with a laugh. Then the monk lowered his head to hide his face, for he was weeping...

As he walked back through the streets, his gait was slow and laboured; he had a strange, stupid expression; his demeanour was grotesque and ridiculous; he looked like a drunken man, for he was tottering: his eyes were half closed, his eyelids red and burning, sweat was coursing down his forehead, and he was stammering between his teeth like a man who has had too much to drink, and who has enjoyed more than his share of the festive banquet.

His thoughts were no longer his own; they wandered like his body, without aim or intention; they were tottering, irresolute, heavy and bizarre; his head was as hot as flames; his brow was burning like a blaze.

Yes, he was drunk from what he had experienced; he was weary of his days; he was sated with life.

That day was a Sunday: the ordinary folk were walking through the streets chatting and singing. The poor monk heard the conversations and the songs; he picked up a few scraps of phrases, a few words, a few cries; but it seemed to him that it was always the same sound and the same voice; it was a vague, indistinct hubbub, a bizarre and noisy gust of wind, which buzzed in his brain and oppressed him.

'Look,' said a man to his neighbour, 'have you heard the story of that poor priest of Oviedo, who was found strangled in his bed?'

Here, there was a group of women enjoying the cool of the evening, standing at their doors. This is what Giacomo heard as he walked past:

'I say, Martha, do you know there was in Salamanca a rich young man, Don Bernardo, you know? the one who, when he came here, a few days ago, had such a pretty, finely caparisoned black mule, and who made her paw the cobbles; well! poor young man, they told me this morning, at church, that he was dead!'

'Dead?' said a girl.

'Yes, child,' answered the woman; 'he died here, at St Peter's hostel. At first, he felt a pain in his head; then, he had a fever, and, four days after, he was buried.'

Giacomo heard others chattering too. All these memories made him tremble, and a smile of ferocity came and lingered on his lips.

The monk returned home, exhausted and ill; he lay on the ground under the bench of his counter and slept; his breast was oppressed, a raucous hollow sound came from his throat; he awoke with a fever, a horrible nightmare had drained his strength. It was night then, and eleven o'clock had just chimed from the neighbouring church. Giacomo heard shouts: 'Fire! fire!' He opened his windows, went out into the streets, and there indeed he could see flames rising over the rooftops. He returned home, and he was about to take his lamp to go into his shop, when he heard, outside his windows, men running past saying: 'It's on the Royal Square, there's a fire at Baptisto's.'

The monk shuddered, laughter exploded from the depths of his heart, and he made his way with the crowd to the bookseller's house. The house was on fire, the flames were rising high and terrible, and, driven by the winds, they were leaping up towards the fine blue Spanish sky that hung over the agitation and tumult of Barcelona, like a veil covering tears.

A half-naked man could be seen; he was grief-stricken, tearing out his hair, rolling on the ground blaspheming God and howling with rage and despair. It was Baptisto. The monk contemplated his despair and his cries with calm and contentment, with the ferocious laughter of the child laughing at the torture of the butterfly whose wings he has ripped off.

In an elevated apartment, flames could be seen burning a

few bundles of paper. Giacomo took a ladder, leant it against the blackened and tottering wall. The ladder shook beneath his steps; he ran up it, reached that window. Damnation! it was just a few old books from the shop, without value or merit. What could he do? He had gone in. He had either to go on through that fiery atmosphere, or come back down the ladder whose wood was starting to get hot. No! he went on.

He crossed several rooms; the floor was trembling beneath his feet, the doors fell in when he approached them, the joists collapsed around his head. He ran through the middle of the fire, panting and furious. He had to have that book! he had to have it or die! He didn't know which way to run, but he kept going; finally, he arrived in front of a partition that was intact, he kicked it in, and saw a dark, narrow apartment. He felt his way around, felt a few books under his fingers; he touched one, seized it and ran from the room with it. It was the one! the *Mystery of Saint Michael*! He retraced his steps, like a man in a dazed delirium. He jumped across the holes, he flew between the flames, but he could not find the ladder he had put up against the wall; he reached a window and climbed down out of it, clinging with hands and knees to the curves. His clothes were starting to catch fire and, when he arrived in the street, he rolled in the gutter, to extinguish the flames burning him.

A few months passed by, and no one heard any more of the bookseller Giacomo, except as one of those strange and singular men the multitude laughs at in the streets, unable to understand their passions and eccentricities.

Spain was preoccupied with graver and more serious

matters, an evil genius seemed to be weighing down on her. Every day, new murders and new crimes, and it all seemed to come from an invisible, hidden hand; there was a dagger hanging over every roof and every family; there were people suddenly disappearing, without leaving any trace of the blood that had flowed from their wounds; a man would set out on a journey, and not return.

No one knew what was the cause of this horrible scourge; for misfortune must be traced to someone else, but good fortune to oneself.

Indeed, there are days that are so ill-fated in life, periods so disastrous for men that, not knowing whose head to call down their curses on, people cry out to heaven. It was in periods that brought unhappiness to the populace that there was a strong belief in fate.

An alert and zealous police had tried, it is true, to discover the author of all these misdeeds. Hired spies had gained entry to every house, had listened to every word, heard every cry, observed every glance, and had learnt nothing. The prosecutor had opened every letter, broken all seals, searched every corner, and had found nothing.

One morning, however, Barcelona had taken off its mourning dress to go and pile into the halls of Justice, where sentence of death was about to be passed on the one who was alleged to be the author of all these horrible murders. The populace hid its tears in convulsive laughter; for when you suffer and weep, it is a consolation, admittedly a selfish one, but in the last analysis quite real, to see other sufferings and other tears.

Poor Giacomo, so calm and so peaceable, was accused of burning down Baptisto's house and stealing his Bible.

He was also accused of a thousand other crimes. So there he was, sitting in the murderers' and brigands' dock, he, the honest bibliophile, he, poor Giacomo, he who only ever thought of his books, was thus implicated in the mysteries of murder and the scaffold.

The room was thronged with people. Finally, the prosecutor rose and read out his report; it was long and diffuse; it was barely possible to make out the main story from the parentheses and reflections. The prosecutor said that he had found, in Giacomo's house, the Bible belonging to Baptisto, since this Bible was the only one in Spain. Now it was probable that it was Giacomo who had set fire to Baptisto's house, to get his hands on this rare and precious book. He stopped speaking and sat down, out of breath.

As for the monk, he was calm and peaceful, and did not deign to glance at the multitude hurling insults at him.

His lawyer rose, he spoke at length and with eloquence. Finally, when he thought he had shaken his audience, he lifted his robe and drew from it a book; he opened it and showed it to the public: it was another copy of that same Bible.

Giacomo cried aloud, and fell back onto his seat in the dock, tearing out his hair. It was a critical moment, everyone was awaiting a word from the defendant, but not a single sound emerged from his mouth. Finally, he sat down, looking at his judges and his lawyer like a man just awakening. He was asked whether he was guilty of having set fire to Baptisto's house.

'No, alas!' he replied.

'No?'

'But aren't you going to sentence me? Oh! sentence me,

I beg you! life is a burden to me, my lawyer has lied to you, don't believe him. Oh! sentence me, I killed Don Bernardo, I killed the priest, I stole the book, the unique book, for there are not two copies in the whole of Spain. My lords, kill me, I am a wretch.'

His lawyer came up to him, and said, showing him that Bible:

'I can save you, look!'

'Oh! to think I believed it was the only one in Spain!' Giacomo took the book and gazed at it: 'Oh! tell me, tell me that you have deceived me. My curse on you!'

And he fell down in a faint.

The judges came back and pronounced his death sentence. Giacomo heard it without flinching, and he appeared even calmer and quieter. He was told there was still hope if he would ask for a reprieve from the Pope, it would perhaps be granted to him. He refused, and merely asked for his library to be given to the man who had the most books in Spain.

Then, when the populace had filed out, he asked his lawyer to be kind enough to lend him his book. The lawyer handed it to him.

Giacomo took it lovingly, shed a few tears on the dog-eared pages, angrily tore it up, and then hurled the pieces into his defender's face, saying to him:

'You lied, friend lawyer! I did tell you that it was the only one in Spain!'

1. Where this translation reads 'earth' in the phrase 'to that earth of ice', there is a word missing in Flaubert's original text.

2. Houris are the virgins of the Muslim paradise, promised as wives to true believers in the Koran. Here, simply, a beautiful woman.

3. Goethe's *The Sorrows of Young Werther* (1774) and Byron's *Childe Harold's Pilgrimage* (1812–18) and *The Giaour* (1813), like *Hamlet* and *Romeo and Juliet*, feature melancholy, alienated, or lovelorn young protagonists.

4. Molière, playwright and actor, makes this comparison in Act 2, Scene 3 of his *L'Ecole des Femmes*, 1662.

5. Antony is the name of a typically romantic hero, and the protagonist of the play of the same name by Alexandre Dumas *père* (1831).

6. Clément Marot (1496–1544) was a French poet who enjoyed great popularity in the sixteenth century. This quotation is taken from the first two lines of his epigram 104, entitled 'Du Beau Tetin'.

7. Ernest is a direct reference to Flaubert's close friend and correspondent, Ernest Charpentier.

8. Lovelace is the handsome, dashing rake in Samuel Richardson's epistolary novel, *Clarissa, or The History of a Young Lady* (1748). Lovelace initially courts Arabella Harlowe, but later transfers his affections to her younger sister, Clarissa. The comparison enhances the notion of Flaubert's madman as a prematurely jaded roué.

9. Carlism was a Spanish counter-revolutionary movement originating in support of Don Carlos, the brother of King Fernando VII. It was adopted in France to describe the supporters of the reactionary French King, Charles X, who derived much of his support from the traditionalist Catholic clergy.

BIBLIOMANIA

1. It is uncertain how much Flaubert knew about Barcelona at the time of his writing 'Bibliomania.' His 'Place Royale' certainly has an equivalent in the Plaça Reial, but his 'barrière des Arabes' or 'Gate of Arabs' is more problematic. He might have had the Catalan barrì ('district') in mind, but unlike other Spanish cities, Barcelona has no Moorish quarter.

2. The *Chronique de Turpin* is a book that does exist, and, in 1835, a new edition reproducing the text of 1527 was published in Paris. It is not known whether Flaubert knew of the work when writing this story.

BIOGRAPHICAL NOTE

Gustave Flaubert was born in Rouen in 1821, the son of a renowned surgeon and physician. In early life Flaubert demonstrated a love for history and literature, and went on to study law in Paris, where, among others, he made the acquaintance of the writer Victor Hugo. A subsequent attack of epilepsy caused Flaubert to abandon his legal studies, but this change of direction was to give him the freedom and solace he desired to concentrate on his writing, over which he laboured painstakingly, and for which he even broke off his much-celebrated love affair with Louise Colet. Following his father's death in 1846, Flaubert lived in Croisset, occasionally travelling to exotic locations such as Egypt, Turkey, and also Tunisia, where he undertook research for his richly detailed second novel, *Salammbô*.

His first published novel, *Madame Bovary*, appeared in 1857, and had taken him five years to write. It immediately provoked a public outcry for its seeming lack of morality. Despite this reaction, Flaubert found himself increasingly respected and admired in artistic circles, and was a regular guest at literary gatherings in Paris. He went on to pen a number of highly acclaimed works – including *Sentimental Education*, his most ambitious work, published in 1869, and *Three Tales*, published in 1877. It is both for his novels and for his remarkable correspondence (detailing his ideas on the life of the artist and the act of writing) that he has been hailed as a true master of nineteenth-century fiction. Flaubert died in 1880.

Andrew Brown studied at Cambridge, where he taught French for many years. He now works as a freelance teacher and translator. He is the author of *Roland Barthes: the Figures of Writing* (OUP, 1992), and various translations of works relating to French history and philosophy.

HESPERUS PRESS – 100 PAGES

Hesperus Press, as suggested by the Latin motto, is committed to bringing near what is far – far both in space and time. Works written by the greatest authors, and unjustly neglected or simply little known in the English-speaking world, are made accessible through new translations and a completely fresh editorial approach. Through these short classic works, each little more than 100 pages in length, the reader will be introduced to the greatest writers from all times and all cultures.

For more information on Hesperus Press, please visit our website: **www.hesperuspress.com**

To place an order, please contact:
Grantham Book Services
Isaac Newton Way
Alma Park Industrial Estate
Grantham
Lincolnshire NG31 9SD
Tel: +44 (0) 1476 541080
Fax: +44 (0) 1476 541061
Email: orders@gbs.tbs-ltd.co.uk

SELECTED TITLES FROM HESPERUS PRESS

Alexander Pope *Scriblerus*
Ugo Foscolo *Last Letters of Jacopo Ortis*
Anton Chekhov *The Story of a Nobody*
Joseph von Eichendorff *Life of a Good-for-nothing*
Mark Twain *The Diary of Adam and Eve*
Giovanni Boccaccio *Life of Dante*
Victor Hugo *The Last Day of a Condemned Man*
Joseph Conrad *Heart of Darkness*
Edgar Allan Poe *Eureka*
Emile Zola *For a Night of Love*
Daniel Defoe *The King of Pirates*
Giacomo Leopardi *Thoughts*
Nikolai Gogol *The Squabble*
Franz Kafka *Metamorphosis*
Herman Melville *The Enchanted Isles*
Leonardo da Vinci *Prophecies*
Charles Baudelaire *On Wine and Hashish*
William Makepeace Thackeray *Rebecca and Rowena*
Wilkie Collins *Who Killed Zebedee?*
Théophile Gautier *The Jinx*
Charles Dickens *The Haunted House*
Luigi Pirandello *Loveless Love*
Fyodor Dostoevsky *Poor People*
E.T.A. Hoffmann *Mademoiselle de Scudéri*
Henry James *In the Cage*
Francesco Petrarch *My Secret Book*
D.H. Lawrence *The Fox*
Percy Bysshe Shelley *Zastrozzi*